"Too bad you can't be around all the time,"

Summer told David.

"Under the circumstances, I can't stay here at night, but there is one solution. You and I could get married and all be one happy family."

Summer's heartbeat sped up at the suggestion, which surprised her, but she knew David was joking as he often did.

"I think we can manage better than that...."

She stood up, and in the darkness she didn't see the stupefied look on David's face. He was surprised at himself. What would he have done if she'd taken him up on his offer?

Books by Irene Brand

Love Inspired

Child of Her Heart #19
Heiress #37
To Love and Honor #49
A Groom To Come Home To #70
Tender Love #95
The Test of Love #114
Autumn's Awakening #129
Summer's Promise #148

IRENE BRAND

Writing has been a lifelong interest of this author, who says that she started her first novel when she was eleven years old and hasn't finished it yet. However, since 1984, she's published twenty-four contemporary and historical novels and three nonfiction titles with publishers such as Zondervan, Thomas Nelson, Barbour and Kregel. She started writing professionally in 1977 after she completed her master's degree in history at Marshall University. Irene taught in secondary public schools for twenty-three years, but retired in 1989 to devote herself to writing.

Consistent involvement in the activities of her local church has been a source of inspiration for Irene's work. Traveling with her husband, Rod, to forty-nine of the United States, Hawaii excepted, and to thirty-two foreign countries has also inspired her writing. Irene is grateful to the many readers who have written to say that her inspiring stories and compelling portrayals of characters with strong faith have made a positive impression on their lives. You can write to her at P.O. Box 2770, Southside, WV 25187.

Summer's Promise
Irene Brand

Published by Steeple Hill Books™

STEEPLE HILL BOOKS

Steeple Hill™

ISBN 0-373-87155-4

SUMMER'S PROMISE

Visit us at www.steeplehill.com

Printed in U.S.A.

But grow in the grace and knowledge
of our Lord and Savior Jesus Christ.
To him be glory both now and forever! Amen.
—*2 Peter* 3:18

To the participants in
Harmony's Thursday night special Bible study
and their continued spiritual maturity.

Chapter One

Carrying one small piece of luggage, Summer Weaver deplaned in Scranton, Pennsylvania, hurried out of the terminal and hailed a taxi to take her to the hospital. Four hours earlier she'd learned that her sister, Spring Brown, had been in an automobile accident and was in critical condition. The hospital's main reception area had closed at ten o'clock, and the driver took her to the emergency entrance. In an unsteady voice, Summer asked for directions to her sister's room.

Summer took an elevator to the second floor and diffidently approached the nurses' station. A few staff members worked intently at computers, but other employees leaned on the counter, chatting aimlessly. They ignored her.

In desperation, Summer stammered, "I'm Spring Brown's sister. Where's her room?"

That statement got their attention in a hurry, and a nurse rushed to her side. "Right this way," the nurse said and hurried down the hall with Summer, suitcase rolling behind her, hustling to keep up.

"How is she?" Summer whispered.

The nurse shook her head. Her expression was grave. "Not good. No one knows what caused the accident but the car plunged over a steep embankment. They had to use Jaws of Life to remove your sister and her husband from the wreckage."

When she entered the room, Summer couldn't believe the patient surrounded by medical equipment and tubes was her sister. The woman's head was bandaged until only the middle portion of her pain-marked, ashen face was visible, but a few tendrils of auburn hair, characteristic of the Weaver sisters, had escaped the bandages and identified the woman as Spring Brown. Her eyes were closed.

"She has severe head bruises and abrasions, as well as internal injuries," the nurse explained as she checked the equipment. Spring's breathing was uneven and labored.

"Is she going to get better?"

The nurse shook her head. "Not unless God sees fit to heal her. We've done all we can do. Perhaps you'd better pray and ask God for a miracle," the nurse said, patting Summer's shoulder as she left the room.

Summer stumbled to the nearest chair. If that's what it took to save her sister, she wouldn't be any help at all, for Summer had never asked God for anything.

She moved the chair close to the bed, and mindful of the tubes attached to Spring's body, Summer gently lifted her sister's hand.

"Spring," she said, "can you hear me?"

The patient's eyelids flickered and Summer raised her voice. "Spring. Talk to me."

Spring's eyes opened a slit, and she smiled. "Summer! How'd you get here? Are Mother and Daddy with you?"

"They're at home in Ohio with the kids. Daddy telephoned and asked me to come since I'm close. It didn't take long for me to get here from New York."

Tears slipped from Spring's eyelids. "Have you heard that Bert died in the accident?"

Summer nodded and squeezed Spring's hand.

"I'm dying, too, but I don't care. Without Bert, I don't want to live."

Summer had never been in love, and she couldn't understand loving a man so much you'd not want to live if he died. Why wouldn't Spring want to get well for her children?

"What about Nicole and Timmy? They need their mother."

Spring shook her head and winced with pain. "You can take care of them."

Impossible! Summer thought, but she wouldn't argue with her sister now.

"I want to be buried at home," Spring rambled on. "When we were on mission assignment in Bolivia, there was never a day I didn't think about the green fields of Ohio. When I was a kid, I always thought of our large white house as a fortress guarding our family. And tonight, I've been thinking about the times when the two of us, and our little sister, Autumn, rode on the big black wagon when Daddy entered his Belgians in competition."

"We did have lots of fun, but I never enjoyed the farm like you and Autumn did. I like living in a big city. I'd probably never go to the farm except to see our folks.''

Spring choked, and Summer started to ring for a nurse when her sister swallowed and coughed. Summer took a tissue from the table and wiped blood from her sister's lips.

''You ought to rest now.''

''Will you take Timmy and Nicole?''

The words astonished Summer, and she felt as if a giant hand were strangling her. ''What! I don't know how to take care of children. Besides, you're going to get well so you can look after them yourself.''

''Promise me!''

Summer was stunned to silence. She couldn't have spoken if she'd wanted to.

''Promise me!'' Spring's voice sharpened. She sounded exactly like their mother, Clara Weaver, and Summer had never disobeyed that voice.

''All right,'' she whispered reluctantly, hoping she wouldn't be held to a promise made under such duress.

Spring smiled contentedly, then her feverish eyes dulled, and she seemed to have trouble focusing on Summer's face. ''Pray for me. I'm a little afraid.''

Summer gasped, but she was willing to try anything to ease her sister's mental and physical suffering.

After a few false starts, Summer closed her eyes, and addressed God for the first time in her life. ''God, you don't know me for I've never talked to You before. I don't even know how to go about this, but Spring needs You, God. Will You give her peace of mind and comfort of heart? I'm glad I'm here with her, but I don't know what to do. Maybe I need You, too.''

Summer sensed another presence in the room, and embarrassed, she looked around to see who'd heard her praying, but she was still alone with her sister. Spring's face, that had been distorted with pain, relaxed into a smile of contentment, and Summer thought she'd gone to sleep. Had God answered her prayer? Was His Spirit in the room comforting Spring? It was a startling thought!

Time passed slowly. Spring didn't rouse, although the nurses checked her frequently, sometimes changing the IVs or adding medication to the tubes. The chaplain came in after midnight, and he held Spring's hand and prayed. When Summer compared his beautifully worded prayer with her miserable effort, she wondered if her petition had done any good.

Spring's breathing increased in irregularity, and Summer was afraid to be alone with her sister when she died, but she didn't ask a nurse to stay with her. Thinking it might ease Spring's mind and bring courage to herself, Summer picked up a pamphlet the chaplain had left and read aloud.

'' 'Precious in the sight of the Lord is the death of his saints.'''

'' 'Even though I walk through the valley of the shadow of death, I will fear no evil, for You are with me.'''

If God was here for Spring as she went through the valley of death, wouldn't He also be with anyone else in the room? Although Summer could only imagine what the presence of God could mean, she had observed the difference His indwelling Spirit had made in her sisters' lives. For the first time, Summer coveted the peace Spring and Autumn had found.

If God was watching over Spring, she might as well try to relax, so Summer leaned back in the chair and closed her eyes. She was startled when she felt a soft hand on her shoulder. Her eyes opened wide as she looked at the bed to see if Spring still lived before she turned to the man at her side. Expecting an aide or a doctor, she was surprised to see a lithe, wiry young man with short dark-brown hair and snappy brown eyes, dressed in a brown business suit. For a moment his identity eluded her, until a two-year-old memory flooded her mind.

David Brown—Bert's brother!

"Summer?" David said.

"Yes, it's me." David was Spring's brother-in-law, and since none of her immediate family was with her, Summer welcomed David. She pulled another chair close to the bed and invited him to sit down.

"I'm sorry about Bert," she said.

Sorrow clouded David's brown eyes. "He was my only brother." He cleared his throat and spoke with difficulty. "Is Spring going to make it?"

"The doctors don't expect her to live. She's been getting worse since I got here about ten o'clock."

"Any of your family with you?"

Summer shook her head. "Spring and Bert left their kids with Mother and Daddy while they went on this fund-raising trip for their school in North Carolina, so my folks have to look after them. Mother isn't able to travel anyway. My sister, Autumn, is expecting a baby any day, so she can't be here. Daddy asked me to come and check out the situation. I live in New York, so it didn't take long for me to get here."

A half smile played around his generous, well-cut mouth. "I remember you intended to move to New York. How do you like living in a big city?"

"It's great," she said, and her blue eyes gleamed with delight. "I've been there almost two years, and I know it's the place for me. I'm working in a Wall Street bank." Her eyes darkened when she remembered the situation. "Did any of your family come with you?"

"No. My parents are really torn up by Bert's death, and they asked me to come and help Spring make funeral arrangements. Is she able to make decisions?"

"She talked for a little while, and she said she wanted to be buried in the Weaver cemetery on the family farm in Ohio."

Perhaps the sound of David's tender, smooth voice had penetrated Spring's subconsciousness and reminded her of her husband, for she opened her eyes.

"Bert," she whispered weakly.

Summer quickly stood and put her hand on Spring's shoulder. "Bert isn't here, dear, but David came."

"I remember now—Bert died in the accident." Spring swallowed with difficulty, and although the Weaver family didn't habitually display overt affection, Summer bent to kiss her cheek.

"Take Bert and me home to be buried."

"Dad wanted me to bring Bert's body to Tennessee," David said quietly to Summer, "but I guess the decision should be up to Spring."

"David," Spring whispered in a faltering voice. He leaned over the bed. "Timmy and Nicole."

"Yes," David said, "what about them?"

"Timmy and Nicole," Spring said again, agitation marking her voice.

"Your kids are in Ohio," David said.

"No. North Carolina," Spring insisted weakly, and she didn't speak again.

The nursing staff had been in and out of the room all night, but David and Summer were alone when Spring breathed her last. A piece of equipment emitted a shrill whistle, shattering the quiet of the room, and Summer screamed. The pressure of the long hours since she'd learned of Spring's accident had been too much, and she started trembling. When two nurses ran into the room, David drew Summer into the hallway and encircled her in the protective cover of his arms. He massaged her back lightly until she stopped trembling, then led her to a small waiting room near the elevator, sat down with her, his arm still around her shoulders.

For a moment she rested against his firm body, then she moved away from him. Her features were composed and she wasn't crying, but David knew he had to take her away from this area before they removed Spring's body.

"We've got to make a lot of decisions in the next few hours," he said. "I'm not hungry, but it might be a good idea to eat breakfast before we tackle the difficult stuff."

"I'll have to call my family first, and I dread it," Summer said wearily.

"Would you rather I talked to them?"

She shook her head. "I'll telephone my sister and let her tell my parents. They've always been so proud of their *three* daughters, and I can't stand to tell them there are only two of us now."

Summer placed the call from a phone booth near the cafeteria. She was relieved when her brother-in-law, Nathan Holland, answered the phone rather than Autumn. Summer didn't know Nathan very well, but he'd made Autumn happy, and Summer was sure he would break the news gently.

After she gave him the bad news, Summer commented on the emotional effect this would have on her parents.

"Landon and Clara will be okay," Nathan assured her, "but I'm worried about the kids. How can we explain to Nicole and Timmy that their parents aren't coming back? Who's going to take care of them?"

Summer's senses reeled when she realized they might be her children now. *God in Heaven, if there is such a Being, what am I going to do with two children whom I've only seen a few times?*

While David talked to his parents, Summer sat with closed eyes, her head in her hands. How could she be so selfish to worry about the effect Spring's death would have on her? Waiting for David to finish, she sincerely mourned the death of her sister, remembering how Spring had looked after Summer on her first day in school—a role Spring had continued all the way through high school. If Summer needed any help, she could count on her older sister. Perhaps she'd partly repaid Spring if she'd made her dying moments easier by promising to look after her children. Summer had no idea how she could keep her promise, but she hoped she would have the courage to try.

When he walked away from the telephone, David took a handkerchief from his pocket, wiped his eyes and blew his nose. From a face marked with sorrow, he gave her a twisted smile.

Summer placed her hand on David's forearm. "It's rough, isn't it? Thanks so much for being here, David. I couldn't have handled Spring's death alone, but it's been easier since you came. I'm just glad our parents didn't have to experience this."

David clasped her hand in both of his. "You're right. I've been wondering why God would let this happen to two people who had dedicated their lives to His service. I still don't know the answer to that one, but I am pleased I could be here for Spring's last few hours. That's what Bert would have wanted. But I wish she'd lived long enough to tell me what she was trying to get across about Nicole and Timmy."

They entered the cafeteria where Summer picked up a bowl of fruit, a cinnamon roll and a glass of milk. David took scrambled eggs, hash browns, bacon, biscuits and coffee. When they were seated, Summer eyed his tray incredulously.

"How can you eat so much food and remain slender as a fence post?" she asked.

"Because I stay active. My job requires a lot of moving around and I work out in gyms regularly." He looked admiringly at her blue eyes and reddish-brown hair. She was slender and petite, about five-and-a-half feet tall. "You're not overweight."

"It's in our genes, I guess. None of the Weavers gain much weight. What job do you mean? Aren't you still in the Air Force?"

"After ten years in the service, I'd had enough. I resigned last year. I'm a detective in Atlanta now."

As David steered her through the next two days of signing documents relating to the deaths of their siblings and contacting a local mortician to arrange for shipping the bodies to Ohio by air, Summer wondered how she could ever have managed without him. She noticed things about David that she'd forgotten—his friendly personality, and his slim, vibrant body as he walked confidently through life as if he didn't have a care in the world.

She was mentally exhausted by the time they boarded a plane for Pittsburgh, where they changed planes for a flight to the Columbus International Airport. She couldn't imagine how difficult it would have been if she had endured the past few days alone.

She'd appreciated David's company, but she had been on edge fearing he would mention their previous meeting or ask why she hadn't answered his letters. It had been rude of her not to reply, but she'd been busy finishing her college education, and David was a complication she didn't want to deal with. After her education had been delayed for several years while she cared for her mother, she had focused on her career. Should she apologize? As she looked out the window, catching an occasional glimpse of a small town or a farmstead surrounded by fields of corn, she recalled the first time she'd met David Brown.

Two years before when her sister, Autumn, had been married to Nathan Holland, Spring and Bert came for the wedding, and David had stopped by the Weaver farm to see his brother, whom he hadn't seen for three years. When one of Nathan's attendants had fallen sick, David was asked to take the usher's place.

David made friends easily, and he'd enthusiastically joined in the wedding festivities. Summer and David had been thrown together during the rehearsal and plans for the reception, and they'd conspired to decorate Nathan's truck with tin cans, old shoes and ribbons. Summer's family couldn't believe she'd assisted David in such a stunt, for by nature she was quiet and reserved.

David had stayed with the Weavers for one day after the newlyweds left for a short honeymoon in Niagara Falls and Bert and Spring started for North Carolina with their family. David invited Summer to spend the day with him at one of Ohio's well-known amusement parks. She refused at first. She had enjoyed the prewedding days with David, but his vibrant, outgoing personality, so different from hers, often made her uncomfortable.

But David was persuasive, so she'd gone with him, and to her surprise, they'd shared a wonderful, exhilarating day. For the first time in her life, Summer felt happy-go-lucky. They took several turns on the roller coaster, rode the merry-go-round and other attractions in the children's area. They strolled along the walkways, stopping to watch three blockbuster shows at open-air theaters. They ate hot dogs, french fries, ice cream and popcorn.

David's jollity had brought unfamiliar laughter to Summer's lips. She laughed at David when he won a cap in the shooting gallery, and laughed with him after the cap fell off when they were suspended upside down on a roller coaster. Summer hadn't laughed that much before or since. It had been a thought-provoking day because she seemed like a different person when she was with David, and Summer liked herself the way she was.

Traveling homeward, David had lowered the convertible's top, and after she tied a scarf around her short auburn hair, Summer luxuriated in the breezy ride. They watched the full moon rise above the horizon, and it was dark by the time they reached the farm. They'd stood for a few minutes on the back veranda, leaning against the rail, shoulders touching, looking toward the white gazebo where both Spring and Autumn had been married.

"I've enjoyed today," David had said. "That will give me something to think about while I'm on duty in Germany the next few months."

Summer gasped when he'd leaned forward and kissed her lightly on the lips, and the sudden surge of excitement she experienced was so unexpected that it startled her. She pretended not to be affected, and said, "Thanks for a nice time."

Summer had been kissed often on high school dates, but not one of those kisses had even ruffled her composure. David's kiss stimulated emotions new to her and had ignited a little spark in her heart that had kept her awake most of the night wondering where association with David might lead. When her sisters had fallen in love, they were willing to sacrifice their wishes to be with the men they loved. Summer knew what she wanted, and she didn't intend to let David Brown or any other man interfere with her plans.

David had sent her two letters from Germany, but she hadn't answered, and he hadn't contacted her again. She wanted to put David totally out of her mind, but when she least expected it, she would think about the day she'd spent with David, ending with his gentle kiss.

When the passengers were asked to prepare for landing in Columbus, and David still hadn't mentioned their previous meeting, Summer breathed a sigh of relief. Perhaps their first encounter hadn't impressed David as it had her. During his exciting life in the Air Force, he'd probably forgotten all about her until he saw her a few days ago. That conclusion should have pleased Summer, but somehow it didn't.

Chapter Two

A week later, Summer peered out the window of another plane hovering over New York's LaGuardia Airport. Like a robot, she fastened her seat belt for landing, closed her eyes and winced as she always did when the plane's wheels hit the runway, took her bag from the overhead compartment and deplaned. She wasn't in the mood to wait for a shuttle, so she took a taxi to her Manhattan apartment.

Summer was displeased with her behavior the past week. She wished now that she'd mentioned Spring's request about taking care of the children.

Prior to the funeral, Summer had kept busy greeting family and neighbors who called at the Weaver home, and she had no time to consider how Spring's death would change her life. But as she'd watched the children's woebegone expressions and the fear in their eyes, Summer's heart had been touched by their sorrow, and she'd made little exploratory gestures to see if she possessed any maternal traits. She'd taken them to the florist to choose flowers to put in their parents' caskets, and on the way home, they'd stopped by Autumn's farm so Timmy and Nicole could see the new baby boy, Lannie, born the day after Spring had died. Summer envied Autumn's easy ways with the children, wishing she didn't feel so inadequate when she was with them.

The night before the funeral, after the children had gone to bed, the Weavers and Bert's family had met in the living room of the Weavers' Victorian home to discuss the children's welfare.

"We'll take them," Autumn had volunteered immediately, and Bert's parents had also said they'd be glad to take Timmy and Nicole.

Forestalling any immediate arrangement, David said, "Shouldn't we put off a decision until we learn if Spring and Bert made provisions for the guardianship of their children? If they made wills, I suppose they'll be at their home in North Carolina. I'll try to find out, if you want me to."

"Yes, that should be checked out," Landon Weaver had agreed. "And in the meantime, we'll keep Timmy and Nicole with us. There's no need to disrupt their lives more than necessary until we know what David learns."

Summer opened her mouth to say something then, but if David was right and Bert and Spring had made other provisions for the children, perhaps her promise wouldn't matter. Hopefully, Spring's mind had been rambling when she'd made her request. Summer had volunteered to stay at the farm and help with the children until David could check out the will, but her mother had insisted that she go back to her job.

"You've already missed more than a week of work," Clara Weaver said. "We're getting along fine with the children. You've always sacrificed for your family, but it's time for you to think about your own future. Don't worry about us.''

Three days after the funeral, her father took Summer and David to the Columbus airport where David's flight to Atlanta was scheduled an hour before she left.

After they checked in and cleared security, David said, "Let's get something to drink before my plane leaves.''

Summer agreed, although she was eager to be rid of David as well as everyone else who distressed her. The first time she'd met David, it had taken months for her to erase his memory from her mind, and the longer she stayed around him now, the more difficult it would be to forget him.

At a small coffee shop, Summer found a table overlooking the runway while David brought coffee for himself and a glass of orange juice for her.

David was alert to Summer's moods, and although he understood how the tragic events of the last week would have disturbed her, he sensed she was troubled about something else. She'd hardly spoken on the drive from the farm to the airport, and she'd given a sigh of relief when her father had told them goodbye at curbside and she had entered the airport. Why was she so eager to leave the farm?

She sipped on the glass of orange juice and stared out the window, but David didn't think she was aware of the departing planes. He studied her face speculatively.

"Are you all right, Summer?" he asked at last. She turned her moody blue eyes toward him, as if she'd forgotten he was even there.

"What? Oh, yes, I'm all right. It's been a bad week."

"I couldn't sleep last night, worrying about the kids. It's a terrible experience for them to lose both their parents. I wish I could do something to help, but a bachelor doesn't have any business trying to raise children."

Summer opened her mouth to tell him about her dilemma, for she thought David would understand, but he heard an announcement on the loudspeaker and drained the last of his coffee. "My plane is boarding now. I'll have to go."

Summer walked to the gate with him. Before he got in line, he put his arm around her waist, and Summer's body tingled at the contact. Grinning and arching his eyebrows teasingly, he said, "I've learned you're not very good at answering letters, but how about phone calls? Will you answer if I phone you occasionally?"

Summer's face grew warm to be reminded that she'd ignored his friendly overtures two years earlier.

"I'll answer," she said quietly.

His arm tightened around her waist. "Good. You'll hear from me in a few weeks."

Summer watched David's plane take off before she moped down the corridor toward her boarding gate. She wished she'd had time to tell David what she'd promised Spring, but if he learned how she was fretting over her responsibility, he might be disappointed in her. She didn't want David to have a poor opinion of her.

Back in her apartment sanctuary, Summer was ashamed that she'd even hesitated to do what Spring had asked her to do. She excused her attitude by claiming lack of experience in child rearing. She would make a lousy foster mother. But if she didn't take care of the children, who would? Certainly, her mother wasn't physically able to raise them.

Holding out hope that Spring's mind had been wandering on her deathbed, and that she and Bert had made other arrangements for the future of Nicole and Timmy, Summer resumed her usual schedule. If only she could dismiss from her mind the scene she'd witnessed on the day of the funeral, she could get on with her life.

After the family returned from the cemetery, Timmy and Nicole had gone to the barn to look at the Belgian colts. Summer had watched from the dining room window as the two children returned to the house. Walking hand in hand, they'd stopped in front of the open window and didn't see Summer, who was partially hidden by the draperies. Timmy was crying and Nicole put her arms around him.

"What'll we do, Nicole? We're too little to stay by ourselves."

"Don't cry, Timmy. God will take care of us. God still loves us even if He did take Mommy and Daddy away. He'll send somebody to take their place. You'll see!"

Timmy had looked up at his sister, and a timid smile brightened his tear-streaked face. "I'll bet He will, too." Then his smile faded. "But who else will love us like Mommy and Daddy did?"

Summer should have gone to the children right then and told them she'd look after them, but her feet seemed glued to the floor. The opportunity was lost when Landon Weaver came from the barnyard and invited the children to take a drive with him.

Summer forced herself to resume her normal work routine, and when she was at the bank, she didn't think about the children. It was only when she went home and read e-mail messages from Ohio that her sister's dying request destroyed her peace of mind. If only she hadn't made that promise!

Summer was late getting home the following Friday evening, and the message light on the telephone's answering machine was flashing when she entered the apartment. With a trembling hand, she pushed the play button.

"Summer, this is David Brown. I arrived in New York this afternoon, and I must talk with you." He gave the name of a hotel and a telephone number, adding, "Please telephone as soon as you get home. I'm in Room 908."

Retribution time had arrived. With bated breath, Summer dialed the number and extension.

"David," she said, when he answered immediately as if he'd been sitting with his hand on the phone. "I worked late today—that's the reason I didn't call sooner."

"Bert and Spring did make wills, and I need to discuss them with you. Could we meet for dinner this evening?"

Having a good idea what David would tell her, Summer didn't want to be in a public place when they talked. "It's been a long day, David, and I really don't want to go out again. Why don't you come to my apartment? I'll order some food from the deli on the first floor."

"Suits me. What time?"

Summer glanced at her watch. It was seven o'clock. "Give me an hour." She told him the name of the apartment complex and her number. Replacing the receiver, she sat on the couch and lowered her head to her hands. She didn't have time to mope if she wanted to be ready when David arrived, but she was scared. Surely if Spring had understood Summer's situation, she wouldn't have asked for that promise.

Rousing after a few minutes, Summer telephoned the deli and ordered large servings of chicken stir-fry and fruit salad, for she remembered David had a big appetite. She showered rapidly and put on blue cotton slacks and a white knit blouse. She didn't take time to wash her hair, but she brushed it briskly. Although not given to taking medication, Summer suddenly realized her head was throbbing, and she took a couple of aspirin that she kept on hand for emergencies. If she'd ever faced an emergency, it was now.

She arranged floral-patterned mats on the small table and set two glasses in the refrigerator to chill. She checked to be sure she had enough cheesecake for dessert, and when the deli delivered her order, she put the food in the small oven to keep it warm. She had barely finished her preparations when a buzzer sounded. She pushed a button to release the door when she saw David's smiling face through the peephole.

"Come in, David," she said cordially, although her throat was dry. "Your telephone message surprised me."

He took her hand and squeezed it gently. "Thanks for seeing me on such short notice."

He wore a wine-colored blazer, gray trousers, a brick-striped dress shirt and a silk tie that matched his blazer. David had wide soaring eyebrows and a straight nose. A long profile kept him from being overly handsome, but Summer had never seen a better-groomed man. His short, straight hair, extending backward from a high forehead, was neatly trimmed to his nape. She understood why he would make a good detective, for his brown eyes, steady in their scrutiny, seemed to take in every detail of her apartment and her appearance with one swift glance.

"Can your business wait until we've eaten?" Summer asked. "I had a light lunch, and I'm hungry."

David removed his coat and laid aside the briefcase he carried. "Sounds good to me. I had a meal between Atlanta and New York several hours ago. You've got a nice apartment," he added, as she invited him into the kitchenette.

"My living quarters were pretty bleak when I first came to New York," she answered with a low laugh, "but my recent job promotion came with a large increase in salary, so I moved into this apartment a couple of months ago. I like living here."

David gave her a strange, pensive glance as they sat at the table.

"I hope you like chicken stir-fry," Summer said as she took foil-covered containers from the oven, arranged them on a silver tray and placed it on the table. She set out bowls of fruit salad from the refrigerator. "Would you rather have iced tea or a soft drink?"

"Iced tea, without sugar, please."

During the two days they'd spent together in Pennsylvania, David and Summer had discussed their respective jobs, so there didn't seem to be much for them to talk about now. Suspecting why David had come to see her, Summer wanted to forestall the discussion as long as possible.

David couldn't think of any subject except what he'd come to tell Summer, and how that news was going to burst the bubble she'd built around herself in New York. They'd already covered the weather, so David finally said, "Looks like you've adjusted to city life."

"There really wasn't much adjustment to make. I've always liked to be alone, and it's easy to lose oneself in a big city."

She served him a slice of cheesecake, but didn't take any herself.

"We're different in that way," he said. "I want lots of people around me."

"I learned to find happiness in my own thoughts and company when I was a child. I'm only a year older than Autumn, and she's prettier and more friendly than I am, so she got most of the attention."

Not a hint of jealousy in the statement, David noted, as if the favoritism to her sister hadn't been a problem.

"Don't you ever get lonely?" David asked. "I like people."

"I don't dislike people, but I can be happy alone."

She stood up and said, "May I get you anything else to eat? More cheesecake?"

"No, thanks. I enjoyed the food. And the company," he added with a wide smile. David knew she would be unhappy very soon, and he hoped a little levity might cushion the blow. Summer's eyes were wary, and she didn't return his smile.

After she loaded the dishwasher, Summer refilled David's iced-tea glass and carried it to the coffee table. He sat on the couch and motioned for Summer to sit beside him as he picked up the briefcase and opened it. She perched on the couch, several inches from his side, resembling a fledgling about to leave its nest.

Expelling a deep breath, he said, "I got in touch with the supervisor of the school where Bert and Spring worked, and she found their wills. She mailed them to me, and I was so surprised at the contents that I couldn't think straight for a couple of days. I started to phone you several times, but decided this wasn't the kind of situation to discuss over the telephone, so I booked a flight to New York."

He took two sheets of paper from a legal envelope and handed them to Summer. "This is Spring's will. Since she survived Bert, her will takes precedence, but the requests are identical to Bert's. You'd better read it for yourself."

Summer held the document a few minutes before she unfolded it. David watched her compassionately, wondering what her reaction would be.

Summer waded through the first few paragraphs of the handwritten document, and since this was the only last will and testament she'd ever read, the wording seemed rather archaic.

I, Spring Weaver Brown, a citizen and resident of Madison County, North Carolina, being of sound and disposing mind, do make, publish and declare this to be my last will and testament, hereby revoking all other wills made by me at any time.

The will authorized the executor to pay all debts, then Spring bequeathed all of her estate, both real and personal, to her husband, Bert Brown, also named as her executor. Then the document further specified:

Should my husband predecease me, or die simultaneously with me, I hereby nominate my brother-in-law, David Brown, to be the executor of my estate, and in the event he will not or cannot serve, I hereby nominate my father, Landon Weaver, to serve in that capacity.

Should my husband predecease me, I hereby bequeath the care of my two children, Nicole and Timothy, into the joint guardianship of my sister, Summer Weaver, and my brother-in-law, David Brown. In the event that one of them will not or cannot serve, then I ask that the other one assume custody of my children. I request that all of my assets be placed in a trust fund to pass to the children, share and share alike, upon Timothy's twenty-first birthday.

I further request that my sister, Summer Weaver, and my brother-in-law, David Brown, assume the leadership of The Crossroads, the school my husband and I established in North Carolina, and that they rear our children in that environment.

"Oh, no!" Summer muttered. In her wildest imagination, she'd never expected David to be appointed coguardian of the children. She broke out in a cold sweat, and the room swayed around her. When she rallied, David had his arm around her shoulders, supporting her and wiping her face with a cold, damp cloth. It seemed as if a giant hand had descended upon her chest, and she gasped for breath.

"Did I faint?" she muttered.

"Almost," David said.

"I've never passed out before. Mother taught us that only weaklings fainted—we wouldn't have dared faint around her."

"You had a jolt that would make anyone black out," David sympathized, and recalling the extremity of Spring's request, Summer straightened up quickly.

"Is that paper binding? We don't have to do what they asked, do we?"

"No, because I doubt these documents are legal. I'm sure no attorney would have drawn up wills like this." He took a deep breath and worry lines formed around his eyes. "I haven't thought about anything else for three days, and I've concluded that Bert and Spring discussed what would happen to Timmy and Nicole if something should happen to them. Perhaps they felt compelled to make some provision for their children before they left on that trip."

"Maybe they'd already discussed asking us to be guardians or godparents."

"That's what I think, too, and the accident occurred before they got our consent."

"Would you have agreed to their requests if you'd been asked?"

"I don't think so," he said slowly.

"So you won't do what they've asked you to?"

"I didn't say that. If they'd asked me in advance, I might have refused, but now that they're gone, it's a different matter."

Summer stood, walked to the window and looked out over a small garden situated in the midst of the apartment complex. Several adults sat on benches watching the splashing fountain, a few children played miniature golf, and one young mother strolled along a path, holding her son's hand.

If she didn't keep her promise, who would hold Timmy's hand?

"What'll happen to Timmy and Nicole if we refuse to take care of them? There's no provision for that."

"Since we weren't consulted about their requests, it's my opinion that if we refuse, other guardians can be appointed by the court. I haven't looked into it. I didn't want to discuss their wills with anyone until I talked to you."

Should she tell David that Spring had asked her to take Timmy and Nicole? No one except Spring had heard her agree to do it. Perhaps other family members would be more suited to look after Spring's kids. As inexperienced as she was, if she assumed the care of two children, they'd be unhappy and she would be miserable. No one need ever know that, in a weak moment, she'd promised Spring.

Suddenly Summer's thoughts reverted to the night Spring had died, when she'd had the overpowering sensation that the two of them weren't alone in the room, that God's Spirit had been there to smooth Spring's move from earth to Heaven. If God had been present, He'd heard the promise!

Her decision to tell David was delayed for the time being when he stated, "I can understand their concern for the children, but why would Bert and Spring expect us to take over that school?"

Summer had been so preoccupied over custody of the children that the second provision of the will had slipped her mind. She turned toward David and said in a raspy voice, "I absolutely will not be a part of that. I don't know how to mother two children, to say nothing of operating a school. I couldn't work with a group of wayward teenagers, and that's the purpose of their school. I won't do it."

"That was my initial reaction, too, but let's give it some thought before we make a definite decision. Will you be working tomorrow?"

"No."

"I'm not scheduled to return to Atlanta until Sunday. Let's sleep on it and talk again tomorrow."

"Yes, let's do. I want to get this settled as soon as possible, so I can go on with my life."

"Will noon be okay? I'll bring a pizza for lunch, and we can go out for dinner. Perhaps to a seafood restaurant?"

"Twelve o'clock will be fine," Summer answered, without commenting on his dinner invitation. She didn't want to get personally involved with David, but when he closed his briefcase and stood, Summer still quivered inwardly with shock and anger. Not willing to face the four walls of her apartment alone the rest of the evening, she said, "Unless you have other plans, you might as well stay for a while. I don't want to discuss those wills, but we can watch a movie or something else on television."

Accustomed to Summer's standoffish manner toward him, her request startled David until he realized that Summer was struggling with an uncharacteristic emotion. She didn't want to be alone! He remembered how shaken he'd been when he read his brother's will. He'd had three days to become reconciled to the requests, but Summer hadn't had time to get over her shock.

"Yeah, I'd like that. Thanks for asking," he said, settling back on the couch.

She handed him the remote. "Why don't you run through the menu and find a movie? Make sure it's a comedy or something light. I'm not in the mood for intrigue and drama. While you do that, I'll fix some snacks."

She poured a jar of cranberry-orange juice over ice and emptied a package of Hawaiian trail mix into a bowl. She placed napkins, glasses, and plates on the coffee table while David glanced at her home. If all of Summer's life was as ordered and organized as this apartment, David understood why she had almost fainted when she'd read her sister's will. On the point of being protective of Summer, David wasn't pleased that his sister-in-law had handed her such a dilemma.

They didn't talk much during the rest of the evening as they enjoyed the antics of a lovable dog that wreaked havoc in the household of his human family. It was after midnight when Summer walked with David to the door.

"Try to sleep," he said tenderly. "I know this has been a terrible blow to you—losing your sister was bad enough, without having to decide how to act upon her requests."

"Especially when I feel guilty about not wanting to do what she asked me to."

As he shrugged into his coat she'd taken from the closet, he said, "Don't lose any sleep over it. We'll work something out tomorrow."

"You're taking this calmly enough. Aren't you upset about what they've done to us?"

"Sure. But I've had longer to get used to the idea than you have, and staying awake all night fretting about it won't change things.'' She drew back quickly in surprise when he brushed a light kiss across her lips as he eased out into the hallway.

''Under the circumstances, don't you think we're at least kissing kin?''

David smiled into her surprised blue eyes and strode rapidly down the hallway. In spite of the sorrow over the death of his brother and the disturbing contents of the wills, David was delighted to have a reason to see more of Summer. After she hadn't answered his letters, he'd decided to forget her, but when he least expected it, Summer's image had infiltrated his mind, and he wondered if he'd ever see her again. He was attracted to Summer's beauty, but he was more intrigued by her quiet nature that he believed concealed hidden fires waiting to be ignited. He wanted to be around when that happened.

Chapter Three

After David left, Summer drank a cup of hot herbal tea to settle her nerves. She'd calmed down somewhat during the movie, but David's caress had disturbed her. He'd been bestowing lots of affection on her the past two weeks, and to her dismay, she realized she liked it. Summer had many reservations about agreeing to Spring's request, and not least among them was her hesitancy to be thrown into frequent companionship with David. He was an attractive man, and he was good company, but she had her future mapped out. There was no place in it for David Brown.

Summer changed into a nightgown and went to bed, but sleep eluded her. When she did doze, she dreamed—mostly of Timmy and Nicole and how forlorn they'd looked during their parents' funeral. In her dreams, the children stood with outstretched arms, looking at her with beseeching eyes. After the secure home life she'd known as a child, she couldn't imagine what it would be like to suddenly lose your parents.

Awakening at an early hour, anger and defiance replaced the compassion of her dreams. Summer could empathize with her sister's concern for her kids, but she considered it inexcusable for Spring and Bert to saddle her and David with the responsibility of a school in the hinterlands of North Carolina.

David's bright and cheerful manner, when he breezed into the apartment at noon, irritated Summer. She'd tried to cover up the ravages of a sleepless night with makeup, but she hadn't succeeded for David was unkind enough to say, "I told you to get some sleep."

Lack of rest had made her grouchy, and she said, "Let's get down to business. What can we do about this dilemma we've had dumped in our laps?"

He sat on the couch and stretched his neatly clad legs out in front of him. "What do you want to do about it?"

"I want to ignore it, but I know we can't."

"I've wondered why Spring kept repeating the children's names at the hospital. I've decided she was trying to tell me the provisions of their wills, but she was too far gone to express herself. If we don't accept the responsibility, the decisions are going to boomerang to our parents, none of whom are able to take over."

Stalling for time, Summer walked around the room, adjusting items on the tables. She paused to straighten a wall collage of framed photographs featuring the Weaver sisters and her father's prize-winning Belgian horses.

"David," she began earnestly, "listen to my side of the situation. I wanted to come to New York when

I graduated from high school, but my parents wouldn't let me. When I was of age and ready to strike out on my own, Mother had a stroke, and I went home to take care of her. I was there six years, and now, at long last, I'm in New York with my parents' blessing. I have a good job and a bright future in the financial market. Do you think it's right for my sister to ask me to give up my life to take on her family, her dreams and her ambition? Surely it's time for me to live the way I want to. It isn't fair!''

The forlorn faces of Timmy and Nicole flitted into Summer's mind, but she willed the images into the background.

"Life often isn't fair,'' David answered in a compassionate tone, "and I do understand your position. As a matter of fact, I'm pleased with my life the way it is now. I don't want to change, either.''

She glanced at David quickly. If he felt that way, maybe she wasn't as selfish as she thought she was. "Then you're willing to refuse their requests?'' she asked eagerly.

"Maybe. Since I wasn't consulted about being the executor, nor either of us about their other requests, I don't feel we're obligated. But if I'd told them I'd do these things, I wouldn't back out.''

David breathed deeply, looked at her with troubled eyes, and spoke in a resigned, yet compassionate, tone. "But I can't make this decision on what is legally right or wrong. Love for my brother motivates me more than legalities. If the situation were reversed, and Timmy and Nicole were my kids, would I want Bert to abandon them? It's not an easy decision, Summer.''

The time had come to be honest or live a lie the

rest of her life. She leaned against the latticed divider between her kitchen and living area, and after a long pause, Summer looked him squarely in the eyes and said, ''It's not that simple for me. I promised Spring I'd take care of her children.''

David stared at her, and despite the stress of the moment, she was slightly amused to see his surprise. He was usually on top of every situation.

''In the hospital before you came, Spring asked me to look after her kids, and she was so insistent and troubled, I finally agreed.''

''Why didn't you say so when we were at the farm discussing guardianship of the kids?''

''I intended to, but when you mentioned that they'd probably made wills, I hoped that Spring hadn't been rational when she made the request and that they'd made different arrangements for the children. That's the reason I left and came back to New York as soon as I decently could. Every time I looked at Timmy and Nicole, I felt like bolting. I know absolutely nothing about rearing children. I'm not sure I even like children—I haven't been around them enough to find out. David, I can't do it, and if I don't, it will torment me the rest of my life.''

She sat down again, leaned her head on the arm of the sofa and burst into tears. David hadn't had any experience with crying women, so he didn't know what he should do. He went to the kitchen and rummaged around in the cabinets. Everything was marked and in place, as he should have known it would be. He heated hot water, poured it into a cup and dangled a bag of a spiced tea blend in it.

He placed the cup on the coffee table and went to the bathroom and dampened a washcloth. He sat be-

side Summer and touched her shoulder. "Stop crying," he encouraged. "I'll help you through this."

"But I don't want my family to hate me!" she
wailed.

"Wipe your face and drink your tea. We'll figure
out something."

While Summer alternately sniffed and drank the
tea, he tried to formulate a plan of action. How could
he advise her when he didn't know what to do?

"You're not the only one who's troubled about this
situation," he said at last. "I've got my life ordered
the way I want it, and I've had a few bitter thoughts
about a brother who would write such a will and not
even mention it to me. I'm not good at administration,
but the thing that bothers me more than anything else
is that I'm not spiritually competent to take on Bert's
job."

"I don't understand."

"You know the kind of school they operated, don't
you?"

"Of course. It's a school for underprivileged and
troubled teenagers."

"But it's also a Christian school, and while I was
a practicing Christian when I was a boy, I'm not now.
I haven't read the Bible for years. I can't be an administrator at a Christian school without a solid spiritual commitment. What about your faith? Are you
qualified for this kind of work?"

Summer leaned back and rested her head on the
couch. "My folks didn't take us to church, so I have
very little knowledge of Christianity. Spring became
a Christian when she met Bert, and Autumn and Nathan are active in church affairs. I've always been the
oddball in the family, and it's the same with spiritual

matters. I'd have no idea how to work with teenagers in a mission school."

"And that may be our way out of this situation," David said. "Just because Bert and Spring wanted us to take over their school doesn't mean we can. They were serving under a mission board, and I doubt very much that the board members would allow us to take over the school even if we wanted to."

Summer brightened, and then her spirits drooped again. "But we'd still be stuck with the kids." She gasped and covered her face with her hands. "What a terrible thing to say! Don't I have any compassion at all?"

David sympathized with Summer. When he'd been around the Weaver family, he'd gathered that Summer hadn't received as much attention as the other two daughters. When she'd been a quiet child, it was easy for her to escape notice.

"I haven't told your parents or mine about the contents of the wills, but I'd like to go to North Carolina and look over the situation before I turn thumbs down on it. Will you go with me? What we find there may make our decision easier."

Summer sighed. "When I've just gotten that good job at the bank, I hate to ask for any more time off. But I suppose you're right. Hopefully, my employers will be patient a little longer."

"Let's take a plane to North Carolina, rent a car and drive up in the mountains where the school is located. I've already established contact with the school's supervisor, and after we talk to her, she may make the decision for us. I'll cancel my flight for tomorrow, and we can leave on Monday."

"That might take care of the school problem, but that won't solve the guardianship of the children."

He moved closer to her and stretched his arm around her shoulders. She welcomed his touch as he said sympathetically, "I won't tell anyone what Spring asked you to do. If you decide you can't take on the care of Nicole and Timmy, no one will ever know about your promise."

"*I* will," she said drearily. "So I'll make arrangements to go to North Carolina Monday morning." She drained the last of her tepid tea and lifted the cup. "Bon voyage."

On Monday morning when they landed at the Winston-Salem Airport, David arranged for a rental car, and they headed westward on Interstate 40.

"From what I gathered by reading Spring's letters, this school is located in the boondocks," Summer said.

"Yes, that's true. I've seen pictures of the place. There are two schools in the compound that's located near Mountain Glen, a little town in a remote area of Madison County. An elementary school that's been operating fifty years or so, and The Crossroads, the school Bert and Spring started. Edna Stollard, the woman I talked to, supervises both schools. The mission board that supported Bert and Spring while they were in Bolivia wanted to establish a facility for troubled teenagers, and they asked Bert and Spring to assume the responsibility. It took them almost a year to erect buildings and get the school in operation. I don't think they have many students yet."

As they approached the Blue Ridge Mountains,

Summer delighted in the awesome scenery and momentarily forgot the decisions facing them.

David was amused at her alternate alarm when they climbed a long steep mountain to her delight when they reached the divide, and Summer clapped her hands like a child, exclaiming over the beautiful vistas before them.

"I've seen lots of mountain scenery on television, but you get a whole new perspective when you're right in the middle of the mountains. Our family's traveling revolved around horse shows, mostly in the Midwest. I've never seen anything as spectacular as this," she added, peering out the window at the mountain ranges surrounding them. "Have you?"

He smiled affectionately at her. "Traveling with the Air Force, I've seen lots of mountains—the Alps and the Andes, and even Fujiyama in Japan. Besides, I grew up in Nashville, and our folks took us to the Great Smoky Mountains National Park almost every summer when we were kids. I like the mountains, too."

In David's company, she saw things she never noticed when she was alone, like the flowers along the roadside, cloud patterns, a majestic rock formation or the color of a bird's feathers. She felt *alive* when he was around. Why was she a different person when she was with David?

While they had waited in the New York airport, she took a book from her purse to read as she always did, but David struck up a conversation with the people around them, and before they boarded the plane, he'd made himself and several others happy by showing a genuine interest in them. Although Summer hadn't said a word, she'd laid aside her book to watch

David and the people he'd befriended. With David, she realized there was another world beside the one she'd built around herself. If they accepted the provisions of the will, she would be with David most of the time. Glancing at his serene profile, and remembering how she enjoyed his occasional touches, Summer both dreaded and delighted in the possibility of being David's constant companion.

Observing Summer's enjoyment of the scenery as they quickly covered the miles, David became more and more infatuated with the person behind the quiet facade Summer normally exhibited. What was there about this reserved, serious woman that drew him to her? Although he didn't want to act on the request made by their siblings, he would welcome an excuse to see Summer often.

When they neared Asheville, David fished in his coat pocket and drew out a piece of paper. "Here are the directions I got over the phone from Edna Stollard. We travel northward out of Asheville until we come to Mars Hill. From there, you'll have to guide me."

Several miles beyond Mars Hill, they traveled westward and upward for a few torturous miles on a narrow road until they reached the small town of Mountain Glen. As the altitude increased, and the trees pressed closely on both sides of the road, Summer stopped talking and a look of panic overspread her face.

Located on the side of a mountain, the town contained several houses and a small business section. David drove carefully along the main street until he saw a sign that pointed to Mountain Glen School. Soon they came to an unpaved road that wound uphill for about two miles before they reached a secluded valley. David stopped abruptly at a dead end marker beside a rustic sign marking the border of Pisgah National Forest. The compound consisted of several buildings. To the left was Mountain Glen Elementary School, a two-story brick building at the base of the mountain with two dormitories behind it. To their right, surrounded by a rail fence, stood three frame buildings with a placard reading The Crossroads over the gate.

"The Crossroads!" Summer said quietly. "There aren't any roads here to cross. They should have named it the jumping-off place." Although it wasn't yet four o'clock, the sun had already dipped behind the heavily wooded mountains, and Summer pulled at the collar of her blouse. The mountains she'd admired so much when they were traveling, dwarfed and suffocated her now.

David's spirits weren't as animated as usual either, and he gave Summer a weak smile. "Looks like we've reached our destination."

"Why would anyone want to live here?" she said in a shaky voice. "I thought it was bad enough when Bert and Spring moved to South America. Bolivia couldn't be worse than this."

"You'd probably change your mind if you saw Bolivia."

"I can't understand why anyone would establish a school in this out-of-the-way place. The reality is worse than I expected."

David took her hand and gripped it tightly. "I don't think either of us can understand it. As I told you, I haven't given any thought to my spiritual self for a long time, but I did attend the service when Bert and

Spring were commissioned as missionaries. When Bert gave his acceptance speech, he made a statement I've never forgotten. With tears running down his face, he said, 'I didn't choose to be a missionary. In fact, I didn't want to be one. It's not the life I would have chosen for myself or my family. But one day, the Lord Jesus appeared to me, much like He did to Paul the apostle. As He said to Paul, He spoke to me, 'I have appeared to you to appoint you as a servant and as a witness of what you have seen of me and what I will show you.'''

David swallowed convulsively and his voice was hoarse. "Bert said, 'I couldn't argue with a call like that and responded in the words of Isaiah the prophet, here I am, Lord, send me. Wherever You lead me, I'll go without question.'''

Hot tears stung Summer's eyelids. "You're right. I don't understand it."

"We never will unless we receive a similar call, but as I look around here, I don't see much likelihood of that happening." He turned off the car's engine. "We might as well check out the place."

David stepped out of the car and breathed deeply. "Well, I'll say this, I haven't inhaled such fresh air since we used to vacation in the Smokies." When Summer still sat in the car, he walked around and opened the door for her.

"Let's go," he said gently, taking her hand, "it won't be too bad. Remember, we just came to look."

She stood on trembling legs and pressed close to him. He put his arm around her waist. "I have the strangest feeling that the mountains are closing in on me, blocking my escape, and that I'll never get out of here. That road was terrible. Think what it would be like in winter. I'm afraid.''

David laughed at her. ''What would your mother say to you if she were here?''

Summer grinned wryly. ''She'd say, 'Stop being so foolish and do your duty. Remember you're a Weaver.' ''

David reached in the car and picked up his cell phone. ''I'll telephone your mother and have her talk to you.''

Summer slapped his hand, took the phone and laid it back on the seat. ''Stop picking on me.'' Looking up at the mountains, she added, ''I doubt very much if you *could* make a call out of this valley. Which way?''

David nodded toward the elementary school. ''Miss Stollard's office is in that building. We'll soon learn what she can tell us.''

With heart pounding, knees shaking and a sinking sensation in her chest, Summer turned toward the brick building facing a decision that would chart her course for the rest of her life. She dreaded the outcome.

Chapter Four

A car drove into the compound and stopped behind David's vehicle. The driver honked her horn.

"I'm parked in the middle of the road. I'd better move," David said. With a wide smile, he waved genially to the woman, hopped in the car and moved it closer to the rail fence that surrounded The Crossroads.

By the time they started up the steps, a half-dozen cars had entered the area. A bell rang, the clatter of feet sounded inside the building, and David and Summer hurriedly stepped to one side as twenty or more children ran out the door and down the steps.

A tall, angular woman appeared in the doorway behind the departing children, and she smiled when she saw David and Summer.

"Sorry you got caught in the stampede. I'm Edna Stollard. Are you Mr. Brown?"

David stepped forward and shook hands with her. "Yes, I'm Bert's brother. This is Summer Weaver, Spring's sister."

"I'm pleased to meet you," Miss Stollard said, "but not under these circumstances. The Browns' deaths have been a blow to the staff and students of The Crossroads. Let's talk in my office."

They entered a narrow hallway, where many students were standing beside their lockers, and Edna said, "Most of our students live on campus. The ones you saw leaving live in Mountain Glen, and their families transport them back and forth to school."

The building had a scent that Summer associated with schools—dust, chalk and stale food—reminding her of the elementary school she'd attended in Ohio. Edna motioned them into an office at the rear of the hallway. It was a crowded room with many filing cabinets, but she moved papers from two chairs to provide a place for David and Summer to sit.

Edna Stollard had a round, rosy face, devoid of makeup, and the kindest brown eyes Summer had ever seen. Her straight hair had been dark-brown at one time, but now it was streaked with gray, parted in the middle and pulled back into a tidy bun at her nape. Edna wore a dark-blue cotton shapeless dress and a white sweater. She obviously didn't give much thought to current fashion.

"I'd expected some of the family to come and gather up the Browns' belongings," she said to David, "but I concluded from your phone message that there's another reason for your visit."

David took Bert and Spring's last wills and testaments from his briefcase and handed them to Edna. "As you know, since you witnessed their signatures, Bert and Spring wrote these before they left here a month ago. Did they discuss the wills with you?"

Edna shook her head. "No. The Browns were in a

hurry to leave and they asked The Crossroads' cook and me to witness their signatures.''

"The contents certainly came as a surprise to us, so please read one of them. Bequests are the same in each will.''

David didn't watch Edna as she read. He stood and looked out the window to the campus. Two adults monitored the activities of students playing basketball on an outdoor concrete court, while other children walked toward the dormitories. The buildings were plain, but the natural beauty was hard to surpass. The school compound was situated in a large alpine valley. High mountain ranges surrounded the valley, and yellow and reddish hues tinged the trees at the highest elevations.

Edna cleared her throat, and David returned to his seat. Summer sat quietly, a resigned expression on her face, hands clenched in her lap. She looked vulnerable and uneasy, making David wish he could shelter her from the fallout of their siblings' requests.

Edna glanced at the papers again. "They made some highly irregular requests,'' she said.

"That's the way it appears to us, too,'' David agreed. "Except for the children, it seems that Spring and Bert weren't at liberty to make the requests they did.''

"No, of course not. Appointments to work at this school are made by our mission board. I'm really surprised, for it isn't like Bert to make such an erroneous move.''

"We've figured out that Bert and Spring may have been worried about what would happen if they did die,'' Summer said, "and they wrote these documents before they started on their trip. They probably thought they'd have plenty of time to discuss the provisions with us."

"Assuming the mission board would appoint you to take over The Crossroads, what qualifications do you have to handle this work?"

"Perhaps we should make it plain, Miss Stollard," Summer said, "that we aren't interested in doing what Bert and Spring requested. We're not suited to fill these positions, and they should have known it."

David chuckled. "Summer does have a Master's degree in Business Administration, but we've never worked with children. Both of us have jobs that are important to us, and frankly, we don't want to disrupt our lifestyle." He hesitated before he added, "And neither of us have the necessary spiritual qualities."

"You aren't like your brother and sister?" Edna questioned in her deep, calm voice.

David and Summer shook their heads emphatically.

"Not spiritually," Summer said.

Edna glanced out the window. "Are you planning to spend the night here?"

Summer's face blanched at the thought of negotiating that winding road after dark, but she didn't want to stay here, either. The surroundings intimidated her and she wanted to leave. What had they accomplished by coming to North Carolina?

David looked at Summer for a decision, and she said, "What's the purpose in staying? We aren't interested in coming to The Crossroads even if the mission board would appoint us."

"Miss Weaver," Edna said, "something has to be done with the Browns' belongings. The house belonged to them. It's not part of the school property."

She looked at David. "Since you're the executor, you'll have to settle their affairs here."

"I didn't know they owned the house," David said. "Did you?" he asked Summer.

"I'd forgotten about it, but I believe Daddy did buy the property and finance building the house. He wanted the kids to have a home of their own, rather than to live in a mission house as they had in Bolivia."

"Wherever they got the money, the house and a half-acre lot belonged to Bert and Spring," Edna said.

"It looks as if we will have to stay overnight," Summer reluctantly agreed. "I don't want to return to Asheville for the night and have to ride up that mountain again in the morning."

"Our return plane reservations aren't until day after tomorrow anyway."

"Where are your homes?" Edna asked.

"I live in New York City," Summer said. "David's home is in Atlanta."

"Then I can see why Mountain Glen doesn't appeal to you," Edna said, an amused expression on her face. "Let's go to The Crossroads' cafeteria and eat supper. Although Bert was the administrator over there, I'm supervisor of both schools. I've lived here in Mountain Glen for over forty years."

Summer regarded the woman in amazement. How could anyone have survived forty years' living in this secluded area and still radiate such serenity and optimism? In Edna's character, she detected the same inner strength Bert and Spring had possessed. Whatever made them different, Summer knew it was something she lacked.

As they walked toward The Crossroads, David said

lightly, "We wondered where the school got its name since there aren't any roads to cross."

"The name has nothing to do with the location. Bert chose the name because every teen attending this school comes with difficulties—a broken home, a police record, rejection and many other problems. At this point, they reach the crossroads of their lives, and they either profit by our instruction and trust God to help them live productive lives or they continue to go downhill."

"What's the percentage of success or failure?" David asked.

"The school has only been operating one year, so it's rather soon to determine success or failure. The enrollment is limited to thirty on-campus students. We've had two boys who wouldn't accept our strict rules, so they left. We count those as failures."

The students were already seated at tables when the three adults entered the noisy dining hall, but talking ceased abruptly as curious eyes turned in their direction. More than curious, the residents seemed frightened as Edna said, "Let me have your attention a minute. We've got company—Summer Weaver and David Brown, relatives of Spring and Bert. They have some business to take care of here. I invited them to have dinner with you and to stay overnight."

One boy lifted his hand. "You anything like Mr. Brown, sir?" he said to David. The boy's face spread in a wide smile, but behind the smile lurked a hint of uneasiness. "We're brothers," David said easily, walking to the table and putting his hand on the boy's shoulder, "but I'm not the great guy Bert was."

"You gonna come here to stay? We're afraid we'll

get somebody who won't understand us like Mr. Brown did.''

"We're just visiting today, but don't worry. Miss Stollard will see that you get a good replacement for Bert.''

The boy shook his head. "Nobody could take his place.''

Edna directed them to the serving window, where she introduced the cook, Hallie Blackburn, and Anita Bailey, a student, who gave each of them a filled tray.

"You look like your sister," Anita said to Summer. "She was neat and pretty, too." She eyed Summer's pink pants set. "I like your outfit.''

"Thank you," Summer said, warming to the girl's admiring glance. "Spring and I do...did," she corrected herself with a pang in her heart, "look alike.''

They took their trays to a vacant table, where Edna bowed her head and gave thanks for the food. The tray contained a slice of ham, sweet potatoes, green beans, vegetable gelatin salad, two cookies and a carton of white milk. The food tasted good, but the servings were small, and Summer wondered if this was enough nourishment for teenage boys. None of the students seemed overweight. No doubt the school operated on a limited budget.

As they ate, Edna explained that Bert had been the administrator and the chaplain, and Spring had taught and helped in the office. Two retired couples served as supervisors of the dormitories. Two women and one man took care of the teaching. The older students did the cleaning and yard work.

"All of these positions are volunteer," Edna said, "except for Bert and Spring who were paid a small salary. The cook is also paid, but otherwise, the staff comes on a six-month or one-year volunteer basis.''

''So there isn't any continuity in the educational program,'' David said.

''More than you might imagine,'' Edna answered, ''as long as we had a good administrator.''

It was almost dark when they left the dining hall, and Edna said, ''Would you like to go to the Browns' home now?''

Summer and David exchanged uncertain glances. Summer wasn't sure she was ready for that, but the sooner they settled their business here, the sooner they could leave Mountain Glen and hopefully never return.

''Maybe we should,'' Summer said.

With Edna in the lead, they walked along a narrow forest path with huge rhododendrons and evergreen trees making a canopy over them. Summer experienced claustrophobia again, and she pressed closer to David. He took her hand and held it until they came to a rustic cabin near the mountain's edge. Before they went inside, Edna led them to the front of the cabin where they overlooked a spectacular view to the southwest. A smoky haze hung over range after range of mountains that seemed to extend into infinity. With the exception of a few lights sparkling in the distance, marking the existence of a town, the area appeared as it had before settlers reached the mountains.

''Bert and Spring wanted to bring up their children in this rural setting,'' Edna said sadly, ''but God had other plans for them.''

Two rustic rockers, with a table between them, stood on the porch. An unwashed coffee cup was on the table, just as Bert or Summer might have left it. Inside the house was further evidence that their loved ones didn't know they were leaving home for the last time. A package of cookies lay on the table. Dishes had been washed and placed on a drying rack. Several large logs in the fireplace waited for a spark to ignite them.

The front half of the house contained a combination kitchen and living area. A narrow hall, with a bathroom at the end, divided the rear of the house into two bedrooms. One room held a double bed and a chest. The other room across the hall had twin beds. Stuffed animals were scattered on one bed, which Summer surmised was Nicole's side of the room, for posters of dinosaurs and football players decorated the other corner. The wooden headboard was cluttered with a small collection of dinosaurs.

"One of you can stay here tonight, or we can offer two guest rooms in the dormitory," Edna said.

Reluctantly, Summer agreed to spend the night in the house.

"David," Edna said, "I'll show you to a room in the boy's building."

"I'll bring your suitcase from the car after I move in to my room," David said, closely eyeing the pallor of Summer's face.

She nodded, pulled out a chair from the table and sat down wearily. When he returned a short time later, Summer still sat at the kitchen table, a frightened look on her face.

"It's so dark," she complained. "And I can't hear a sound."

Sitting across from her, David answered with a note

of levity in his voice, "That's supposed to be one of the benefits of country living."

"Perhaps so, but I'm not keen on country living. At the farm, we had several dusk-to-dawn security lights. It never got completely dark except on those times when the power was off, and even then, Mother always had lots of lamps and candles on hand."

"I'll exchange places with you if you like," David volunteered, "but I think you'll get more rest here. The dormitory walls are paper thin, and the boys are rather noisy. I figure I'll want a little peace and quiet before morning."

"I'll be all right." She got up and paced the floor for a few minutes, then she looked in the refrigerator and some of the cabinets, where there was a good supply of food. In spite of the wills they'd left behind, it was obvious that Bert and Spring had intended to come home again.

"You might as well come here for breakfast. There are tea bags in the cabinet and frozen juice and a loaf of bread in the freezer." Her eyes flitted around the room. "David, what are we going to do with their things?"

David shook his head and surveyed the cabin's furnishings. One wall cabinet contained mementos that Bert and Spring had brought from Bolivia. A small television was centered before the couch and a deep lounge chair. An open Bible lay on a desk. Had Bert and Spring sat at that desk when they'd written their wills?

"If I'm the executor of the will, I suppose I can make the decision of what to do with everything, but it won't be an easy task."

David hated to leave Summer alone, but he knew

he should leave. In spite of his good intentions, he figured Edna wouldn't approve if he spent the night in the house with Summer, even if Summer would allow it. He laid a tender hand on her shoulder.

"Try to sleep. I'll be here early in the morning."

When he stepped off the porch, Summer opened her mouth to ask him to stay longer, but she didn't speak. She had to stop depending on David's presence to calm her fears.

Summer showered in a thin stream of tepid water and changed into her nightgown and robe. She couldn't bring herself to sleep in Spring's bed. She picked up a blanket and went into the living room.

She laid the blanket on the couch, wandered around the room and picked up the Bible lying open on the desk. Several lines were highlighted, and she read aloud, "'For I am already being poured out like a drink offering, and the time has come for my departure. I have fought the good fight, I have finished the race, I have kept the faith. Now there is in store for me the crown of righteousness, which the Lord, the righteous Judge, will award to me on that day—and not only to me, but also to all who have longed for his appearing.'"

The minister who'd preached their funerals had read the same passage, and Summer considered it a fitting epitaph for Bert and Spring. She turned the pages of the Bible wondering if it contained any words to guide her in the decisions she must make.

There were many underlined passages, and she paused at one verse marked in Psalm 144, "Happy is that people, whose God is the Lord." Accepting someone as Lord meant He would be the ruler of your life. If she took that step, could she more willingly carry out her sister's request?

Chapter Five

When David approached the cabin the next morning, Summer sat on the front porch wrapped in a blanket staring toward the distant mountains. Her face was unreadable, but he sensed the indecision and the fears she faced. If she moved to Mountain Glen with the children, would it make or break her? She looked so innocent, and he wondered what would happen to her if she chose The Crossroads.

David hadn't slept much because he was fighting his own battles. He didn't want to leave his job, although he felt duty-bound to do what his brother had requested, but only if Summer would partner with him. He believed there was a warm, vibrant person behind the quiet facade she exhibited. If he could be with her a few months, he was certain he would discover the personality she'd displayed when they'd spent the day at the amusement park.

Being in this isolated area, where his brother had chosen to serve the Lord, had caused David to realize how far he'd wandered from God and the spiritual values his parents had taught him. In addition to furthering his relationship with Summer, David longed to find the peace and security he'd once known when he came into God's presence without guilt. He believed he could find it at The Crossroads. David hadn't lived a bad life, but he remembered a Bible verse he'd memorized as a child. "Anyone, then, who knows the good he ought to do and doesn't do it, sins." So he'd erred, not by the sins he'd committed, but by what he hadn't done.

David deliberately stepped on a twig, and when it snapped, Summer's startled eyes turned in his direction. When she started to stand, the blanket wrapped around her legs and she stumbled. He vaulted up on the porch and took her hand.

Clasping the blanket around her shoulders, she said as she entered the cabin, "I'll dress and then we can have breakfast. I have coffee ready. Help yourself."

When she returned to the kitchen, David had poured cups of coffee and glasses of juice.

"I made some toast and found a jar of jelly in the cabinets. No butter," he said.

She sat at the table and spread jelly on the slice of bread. "How'd you sleep?" David asked.

"Didn't sleep at all! There were too many memories floating around in my head. I kept thinking about Spring and her family, and their association to this cabin. It's still hard to accept she's gone."

"I know what you mean. After Bert left for college and then the mission field, we didn't see much of each other, but we were good buddies when we were kids. We didn't fight like a lot of brothers."

A faraway gleam crept into Summer's eyes, and she smiled weakly. "You've met my mother, so needless to say, there wasn't any fighting in the Weaver household.''

After they finished eating, Summer took the dishes to the sink. ''Let's get started with whatever we need to do today. I hate indecision.''

David inclined his head cautiously. ''I have a feeling we aren't going to have all our problems settled when we leave here today.''

She hurriedly washed the dishes, while David dried them and put them in the cabinet.

''It's still too early to meet with Miss Stollard,'' David said. ''She's probably on duty until the students settle into classrooms for the day. Let's take a walk and look at the scenery.''

The morning was crisp, and it was a pleasure to breathe the evergreen-scented mountain air. The sky was cerulean, with a few wispy clouds floating high above the valley. The area seemed less forbidding this morning than it had yesterday. They walked along a path to a small lake. Three deer, grazing in the meadow, flicked their tails and ears and stared at the intruders. The buck stomped a front foot at the intruders when Summer and David paused to watch.

''They're not afraid,'' Summer said.

''No reason to be, I suppose.''

The deer moved away slowly, grazing as they went. Summer and David sat on a concrete bench beside the lake.

After a few moments of silence, David asked, ''I'm having a hard time envisioning myself as a family man.'' He chuckled reminiscently. ''When we were kids, I remember telling Bert that, when I grew up, I intended to get married and have a house full of kids. There were only three of us, and one of my buddies came from a family of ten children. I felt like I'd been shortchanged. Since I wasn't doing anything about it, maybe Bert thought he ought to give me his kids.''

''Why haven't you gotten married?'' Summer asked.

''Never did get around to it. I joined the ROTC in college and went right into the Air Force after I graduated. The years drifted along, and I didn't give it any thought. Maybe I didn't find the right woman.''

''No serious affairs either?'' Summer asked, surprised at her audacity.

He arched his eyebrows. ''You're kinda inquisitive, aren't you?''

Summer colored slightly. ''Why didn't you come right out and say I was nosy? Guess it isn't any of my business.''

''No, I haven't had any affairs—serious or otherwise.'' With a tantalizing grin, he said, ''Now it's my turn. Why haven't you gotten married? You're as old as I am.''

''There are other things I wanted more than marriage. My father's Aunt Naomi never married, and she became my role model. She was one of the first women to get a doctorate in economics at OSU, and she made quite a name for herself in the business world by establishing her own factory to manufacture tack accessories for horses. My parents and grandparents had also been successful in the equine industry, and I suppose I inherited some of their ambition. I decided if Aunt Naomi could succeed in the business world, I would, too.''

''But a lot of successful women combine marriage and a career.''

''Yes, I know, but when Spring and Autumn fell

in love, they were willing to give up everything to be with the men they loved. Of course, Autumn went on to become a veterinarian, but she probably wouldn't have if Nathan would have married her when she was eighteen.''

''I'm surprised some man hasn't convinced you otherwise,'' David said.

''I also inherited a lot of Weaver stubbornness. I'm not easily persuaded.''

''Is that a warning?''

Getting up from the bench, she said, ''Nope—just the truth. I don't know how we got off on this subject, but let's go see Miss Stollard. We have planes to catch tomorrow.''

They heard the hum of voices as they entered the building. Edna was in her office, talking on the phone, so they waited in the hallway. She motioned them into the room when she finished her conversation.

After they sat down, Edna said, ''I've been talking to the chairperson of our mission board in Raleigh. I explained about the wills, and I also told him of your reluctance to take on this work and why. At this time, there is absolutely no one available to administer the work at The Crossroads, and the director is willing to appoint you to work here on a temporary basis, on my recommendation, as long as I oversee the spiritual needs of the children.''

Summer's face blanched and she gripped the arm of her chair. Lacking the necessary qualifications for the work, she'd hoped they would be relieved of the need to make a decision about coming to Mountain Glen. Her last hope had been jerked out from under her! David stood behind her chair and placed understanding hands on her shoulders.

"And what if we don't agree to come?" David asked.

"The school will close at the end of the month."

Alarmed, he asked, "What will happen to The Crossroads' residents?" Summer shuddered beneath his hands.

"They'll be placed in foster homes or returned to where they were before they came here. We'd have no other choice."

Summer gasped. The faces of the youth who'd watched them in the dining room passed through her mind. What would it be like to have no home? No one to love or take care of you? In her youth she'd despaired sometimes at the restraints her parents had put on her, but she'd always felt secure.

"So if we don't accept this work," she said, "we'll not only be guilty of refusing to do what Bert and Spring requested, but we'll also be responsible for dislocating thirty young people?"

"I'm sorry, Miss Weaver. I'm only answering your questions. Our mission organization represents a small group of churches and our finances are limited. If there was time, we might find someone to take over, but on such short notice, we don't have any prospects."

"If we agree to come, we're actually buying time for you and the residents," David said.

"Yes, I suppose that's it," Edna agreed.

A boy pecked on the office door and said, "Miss Stollard, you're needed in room four. One of the girls is sick."

"Excuse me a few minutes," Edna said and left the room.

"Would you be willing to take a leave of absence from your work for a year?" David asked Summer after Miss Stollard exited. "If we come until they find replacements that might fulfill the intent of the will."

"I can't live here, David. I feel suffocated in these mountains. After living most of my life where I can see for miles in every direction, I'd be miserable at The Crossroads."

"You can't see very far from a Manhattan apartment."

She ignored his comment. "Why can't I take the children to New York with me and you take over the administration of the school? That's the most workable solution, and we'd be doing what Bert and April wanted."

That plan had come to her during her wakeful night when she despaired of her increasing dependence upon David. If she returned to New York, and he lived in North Carolina, she would seldom see him. Continued association with David Brown was presenting a problem—she'd almost convinced herself that it would be worth doing what her sister had asked, if she and David could work together, and that wasn't what she wanted.

Her words surprised and disappointed David. The past few days with Summer had been pleasant, and over and above his sense of duty to his brother, he was willing to come to The Crossroads for the opportunity to become better acquainted with her.

"Do you intend to stop work and become a mother to Timmy and Nicole?"

"I doubt that I have any maternal instincts, but

there are excellent nanny services in New York. I can afford to provide a good nanny for them.''

David's eyes narrowed, and Summer sensed he was angry.

''I will not agree to that. Those two kids are grieving, and Spring wanted you to raise her children at Mountain Glen. They need to live in a familiar environment. Don't you feel any responsibility to your own family?''

''I'd be fulfilling my responsibility by taking care of Nicole and Timmy. That's all I promised to do.''

They stopped talking when they heard Edna's deliberate steps in the hallway. Her keen brown eyes shifted from one to the other, perhaps sensing a disagreement.

''I'm willing to come for a year, or until your mission board can make better arrangements,'' David said tersely. ''I can't speak for Summer.''

Summer walked to the window and looked at the playground where children were exercising. Behind The Crossroads' administration building, a tiny dog pulled a tin can from the garbage pail, and while eating the contents, his head stuck in the can. His efforts to remove his head were futile, and the bewildered dog ran in circles until a blond-haired boy hurried out of the building and freed him. Summer was forced to make a comparison. Residents at The Crossroads needed saving from the bondage of past mistakes, either their own or their parents' neglect. Was she the one to set them free?

She turned toward David and Miss Stollard. ''Although I don't want to, I feel compelled to live my sister's dream. I'll give it the best that's in me for a year. I won't commit further than that.''

David's eyes softened and he reached for her hand. Summer eluded his touch, and her blue eyes were frosty when she stared at him. *She's resentful because I wouldn't agree to her request and let her off the hook,* David thought, but he was exhilarated at the prospect of continued companionship with Summer.

Although she was piqued at David, Summer knew they had life-changing plans to make, and she stifled her annoyance. Edna had given them a copy of the yearly budget for The Crossroads, and to keep her mind off the winding, mountainous road they were descending, she studied the figures. When they headed eastward on the interstate, she sighed and said, "Now what?"

"I have no idea what we should do first," David said. "I'm sorry we told Edna we could return in three weeks."

"The sooner the better," Summer said, "for I'm going to be anxious until we're settled in at The Crossroads. It isn't fair for me to ask for a leave of absence, so I'll resign my position at the bank. I'm sure my boss, Mr. Abel, will give me a good recommendation if I ever want to work in New York again, but I'll have to forget New York until my work is done at The Crossroads. If I fill Spring's shoes, I'll have to cut my ties with the past."

David nodded agreement. "I'll resign, too, but I can always find a job at another detective agency or organize my own business when the time comes."

"This is going to come as a shock to our families. Mother and Daddy will have a fit. I intend to resign before I let them know."

"My folks will be glad about it," David said.

"I live in a furnished apartment, so all I'll have to move are my personal items. I'll buy a car and drive to North Carolina. I won't be stranded on that mountain without some means of transportation."

"I'll probably trade my car for a Jeep or some other sport utility vehicle, but I haven't gotten that far in my plans yet."

"The longer we talk, the more I realize what we've gotten ourselves into. How are we going to get the children to North Carolina?"

"I'll drive out and bring them to The Crossroads. But have you considered that in addition to the fact we're both going to be without any income, except that pittance Edna mentioned, we're going to be responsible for the expense of raising two children? Bert's and Spring's wills stipulated that their assets be put into trust funds for the children to draw when they come of age. So if they had insurance, that money will be held in trust and won't do the kids a bit of good now." He paused, and his brown eyes suddenly blazed with anger, an unusual emotion for David. "I believe Spring and Bert had a temporary lapse of mind to ever concoct such documents."

"What *will* we do for funds?"

David shook his head. "Live the same way Bert and Spring did, I suppose."

"Mother sent them money occasionally, but they wouldn't accept much for they said that self-denial was a part of their calling."

"And I don't deny myself anything. I looked over those papers while you went to the cabin and packed," David said and laughed shortly, but there was no mirth in the sound. He flicked the collar of his shirt. "The budget for a day's food at The Crossroads is less than what I paid for this shirt. The more I think about it, I'm sorry I pressured you into accepting their requests."

Summer looked at him curiously. She'd never seen him despondent before, and she stopped being sorry for herself and began to understand what this move would mean to David. If he resigned a good position to become the administrator of a mission school, it would be quite a blow to his ego.

"I've always taken expensive clothing for granted, too. From the time we were old enough to choose our own clothing, Mother took us to exclusive stores in Columbus or Cincinnati to shop. She was still generous with clothing after I came to New York."

"A lot of clothes that probably won't be practical at The Crossroads."

Summer nodded agreement. "When I've had all the money I wanted at my disposal, it's going to be hard to live on a small salary. I wonder if I can get used to it as my sisters did. Spring lived for several years in Bolivia without the latest in fashion, and when Autumn was struggling to get through veterinary school, at times she hardly had enough to eat, so the last thing she worried about was her clothes. Do you suppose I'll come to that?"

David lifted her left hand and kissed her fingers. "I'm sure you'll have the strength to do what you have to. Remember you're a Weaver!"

His joking reminder of the principle Clara Weaver had drilled into her daughters lifted Summer's spirits.

David's plane left for Atlanta an hour sooner than Summer's flight time. She stood beside him as he waited to board, and he said, "Let's tell our parents right away, and then I'll telephone you in a few days." He handed her a card with his telephone number. "You get in touch with me if you need to before that."

"I'll notify my parents by e-mail. If I talk to Mother by phone, she'll try to argue me out of what I've agreed to do. She'll remind me of how much money they've spent on my education and that I'm throwing my life away. I haven't forgotten the commotion Spring stirred up when she came home to tell us she planned to marry a missionary. I only hope I have the strength to stand by my decision as Spring did."

The boarding call for David's seating came over the loudspeaker, and he drew her to one side. "It'll work out okay, Summer. I don't understand why, but it feels right for us to do this. We made our decisions by instinct—perhaps I should say by faith—rather than by logic, but we have to stop doubting and move forward." He put his arm around her shoulder, and she leaned against him. "I'm looking forward to getting to know you better. Will it be so awful seeing me every day?"

Summer experienced that giddy feeling David had inspired when they'd spent the day at the amusement park in Ohio. She put her arm around his waist, gave him an impish grin, and said, "I might be able to bear it."

He dropped his bag on a seat, and quickly drew her into the tight circle of his arms. His eyes brightened with laughter before his lips captured hers in a demanding kiss. For a moment she surrendered to him, consumed by conflicting emotions, before she lifted a hand and pushed him away.

"David," she whispered, "you'll miss your plane."

"I really don't care," he said, laughing softly, as he dropped another kiss on her moist lips, grabbed his bag and hurried down the jetway. Summer pressed shaky fingers against her lips.

How had that happened? She and David had enough problems without getting romantically involved, but she had trouble convincing her heart as, feeling lonely, she walked slowly to her boarding area. It was a strange sensation because normally, she preferred to be alone. She dreaded returning to the apartment where her doubts would surface again. When she was with David, Summer could think rationally about the change in their lives, because he seemed to understand the reason she hesitated to do what Spring had asked. The next few weeks while she prepared to move to North Carolina, she'd have no one to encourage her.

Chapter Six

Summer spent most of the time en route to New York scribbling in a notebook, carefully wording the e-mail message to her parents. But she waited until it was time to leave for work the next morning before she sent the message, so her mother wouldn't have time to call. She didn't want to deal with her parents until she'd given two weeks' notice to her employer.

Mr. Abel tried to persuade her to change her mind, but when he realized she was determined, he said, "You're throwing away a bright future in the financial world. I had great plans for you, Summer, but the qualities that make you an asset to this bank—faithfulness, conscientiousness, and integrity—are the qualities that prompt you to sacrifice your desires for your sister's family."

"It was a difficult decision, but one I had to make. Thanks for understanding."

"I *don't* understand," Abel said, "but you have my best wishes, and I'll do everything I can to help you—now or later. Please keep in touch with me. I'll want to know how you're getting along." He came around his desk and shook hands warmly. "Good luck, Summer."

"Thanks. I'll need it."

The telephone call from Ohio came about eight o'clock, and Summer lifted the receiver anxiously.

"Summer, my poor child," Clara said, and her compassionate tone completely unnerved Summer. This wasn't the reaction she'd expected from Clara Weaver.

"Oh, Mother," Summer said tearfully. "I didn't know what to do."

"You did the only thing you could have done, but I'm so sorry your life has been disrupted again. I don't understand why Bert and Spring would expect this of you, but I believe they thought it out carefully. It isn't like either of them to be inconsiderate. How's David dealing with it?"

"Better than I am," Summer sighed, "but it's a big change for him, too. We both resigned from our jobs today."

"Landon and I will assume the financial support of the children."

"Let us try it on our own first. I've decided to take it a day at a time. That's all we can do. I'll buy a car and drive to North Carolina in three weeks. David will come after Timmy and Nicole soon, but we'll let you know when to expect him. How are they doing?"

"They haven't really comprehended that their parents are gone, but when they get back to their home, and Spring and Bert aren't there, you may have a rough time with them."

"Have you told them that David and I are their guardians?"

"Yes. We thought they should know as soon as possible, for they've been asking what's going to happen to them."

"I'm afraid to ask how they reacted to the news," Summer said in a shaky voice.

"They didn't say much, but they seemed happy to be coming home to North Carolina. Nicole said, 'See, Timmy, I told you God would send someone to take care of us.'"

Summer choked a little when she tried to answer. "I'm afraid I'll make a terrible mother."

"Nonsense! I have no doubt that you'll be very efficient. I'll be praying for you."

"Really, Mother!"

"When we were so burdened with Spring's death, Landon and I asked the local pastor for counseling. We realize now how much we've missed by completely ignoring God's mercy and His will for our lives. We've received comfort that we didn't think was possible, and we finally understand why Spring and Autumn changed after they became Christians. I provided everything for you girls except spiritual training, which I realize now was the most important thing I could have given you. It's always been hard for me to depend on anything except my own will and strength, and more than any of my children, you've inherited that trait from me. I'll pray that you'll learn sooner than I did that there comes a time when we can't go it alone. A time when we have to depend on God and others."

Thinking of how much she was already depending

on David, Summer answered, "I'm already finding that out."

"Good," Clara said. "Landon will talk with the car dealer in Columbus where we buy our vehicles, and he'll make contact with a reputable dealer in New York City. You can go and choose what you want."

"Thanks, Mother, but I won't buy a new car. Most of the young people we'll be working with come from low-income homes. I won't show up with an expensive new car. It would be great, though, if Daddy finds out where I can buy a dependable used car. David intends to sell his sports car and buy a Jeep."

"How are you and David getting along?"

Remembering David's goodbye kiss yesterday, Summer's face flushed, and she was glad her mother couldn't see. "Not bad," she said evenly, "considering how different we are. We've been thrown together in a situation where we have to get along, and both of us know it."

"We love you, Summer," Clara said, and Summer nearly dropped the phone. Her mother hadn't told her that before. Clara Weaver *had* changed!

The conversation gave Summer quite a jolt. Her parents had become Christians, so again she was the oddball of the family—the only one of the Weavers who hadn't embraced the Christian faith. And Clara's statement that Summer was like her mother had also been startling. That couldn't be true! But, was it?

Clara didn't have any close friends—neither did Summer. Clara liked her privacy—so did Summer. Clara was fastidious about housekeeping and in her personal appearance, as was Summer.

Mentally she ticked off, one by one, the traits she shared with her mother, and Summer didn't like the comparison. She couldn't believe she exemplified the things she resented in her mother, but it was true. Only in the matter of domination over others was she unlike Clara. God had changed Clara into a different person. Could He change her as well?

Summer resented how much she wanted to talk to David, but after two nights, and David hadn't called, Summer telephoned him. She got his answering service, surprised at her disappointment. Was David becoming that important to her?

Debating whether or not to leave a message, she finally said. "This is Summer—just wanted to report that I'm no longer employed. The CEO tried to change my mind, and he said I could have a job with them anytime I wanted it." She couldn't bring herself to ask him to return her call, so she hung up abruptly. What had her mother said? That one of the worst hurdles she had to overcome in becoming a Christian was to depend on others. Like her mother, Summer didn't want to lean on anyone, and she resented the tendency to depend on David.

Two more days passed, and she still hadn't heard from David. He'd said he would be in touch soon, so what was the problem? She wished she hadn't telephoned him. Maybe David wasn't happy to be so closely connected to her. Had she been too receptive to his caresses in the airport? She'd lived over thirty years without becoming emotionally involved with any man. Why did she have to start now?

The third night when Summer reached home, the message button was blinking. With shaking fingers, she accessed the message.

"Hi, Summer. David. I had to make a quick trip

out of town. Give me a call tonight. I'll be at home all evening.''

He can just wait on me a while, Summer thought as she went into the bedroom to change her clothes, and she flushed when she remembered that was an attitude she'd picked up from her mother. Before she started dinner preparations, she returned David's call.

''Sorry I ran out on you,'' David said immediately. ''But I'm working on a case I have to finish before I leave the agency. I had a lead that took me to Texas for a few days. I don't use my mobile phone when I'm investigating. So, how are things working out for you?''

''Not bad,'' Summer answered. ''My resignation has been accepted. Mother and Daddy are going to buy a used car for me. I only worked part-time at the bank while I was in school so I haven't saved much money. I'll get a refund on what I've paid into the retirement fund, but it won't be enough to buy much of a car.''

''About all I accomplished before I left town was to turn in my resignation. But I'll get busy right away. When do you expect to arrive at The Crossroads, so I'll know when to go after Timmy and Nicole?''

''I'm aiming toward the first week of October. Will that be convenient for you?''

''Yes. I'll contact Edna and tell her when we'll be there. Are you scared, Summer?''

''I'm in shock more than anything else,'' she said with a slight laugh, ''but it helped when my parents accepted it so well. I thought Mother would try to change my mind, but she was very understanding. She said there was nothing else we could do, and she promised financial support for the kids. I'm trying to take it a day at a time."

"Great! I'll telephone in a few days, but get in touch if you need me." He hesitated. "I'm looking forward to seeing you again."

She felt the same way about him, but the Weaver pride kicked in, and Summer said, "Which won't be very long. Bye, David."

Knowing David was as near as a phone gave Summer a warm feeling, and she set about packing with a lighter heart.

Summer arrived in Asheville in late evening, two days ahead of schedule. She registered at a motel, mindful of her limited income, but also fearful of climbing the mountain after dark. After dinner at a restaurant adjacent to the motel, she returned to her room and telephoned her parents to let them know she'd arrived safely in North Carolina.

To her surprise, David answered the phone.

"David! I didn't expect to get you."

"Are you having trouble?" he asked quickly.

"Oh, no. I wanted Mother and Daddy to know I'd arrived safely in Asheville."

"They took Timmy and Nicole to Woodbeck Farm to say goodbye to Autumn and Nathan. We're leaving early in the morning. You're earlier than you expected, aren't you?"

"Yes. Since I'd never driven so far by myself, I allowed more time than I needed. It wasn't bad at all."

"I'm planning two days for the trip with Timmy and Nicole. If I traveled alone, I'd make it easily in one day, but I have a suspicion that traveling with two kids will slow me down considerably. Look for us sometime day after tomorrow.''

"How are you getting along with the children?''

"I've been here three days making friends with them so they won't feel as if they're starting out with a stranger. We went to the zoo one day, and your dad has taken us on wagon rides with the Belgians.''

"I'll go to The Crossroads tomorrow morning and try to get settled in, so I'll be ready for you. Tell Mother and Daddy I called.''

"You okay, Summer?'' he asked anxiously.

"I think so. I've gotten over my anger, and I'm accepting the situation. I still dread what's ahead of us for I don't know how I'll measure up.''

"You'll be great. Remember you're a Weaver!'' he joked, and then more seriously, he cautioned, ''Be careful on the mountain tomorrow morning. There could be some fog.''

Was David becoming the brother she'd never had? Summer wondered as she settled down in a large armchair. Summer was sure that kiss they'd shared wasn't filial. Was a brotherly relationship what she wanted from him? Summer's fear of losing her independence kept her from answering the question.

A Bible lay open on the table by her elbow, and Summer picked it up. Someone, perhaps a former occupant, had underlined a verse in the book of Hebrews. ''Let us then approach the throne of grace with confidence, so that we may receive mercy and find grace to help us in our time of need.''

She needed help now more than she'd ever needed it. Was help available in this book? Every member of her family, except herself, had apparently found an answer to their greatest needs in the Bible. Summer slowly turned the pages, reading many passages that spoke of God as the Creator.

She laid the Bible on the table and thought about what she'd read. If God had created all mankind, then that meant Summer Weaver was His creation. And if God had created her, didn't it follow that He would be concerned for her and provide her needs? It was a truth too great for Summer to completely comprehend, but it gave her a degree of security as she prepared for bed and turned out the light. If God kept track of His creations, then He knew she was alone in Asheville, North Carolina. But was she alone? According to the Bible, God was not far away from anyone if that person looked to Him, and tonight, Summer's heart was reaching for Him.

By the time Summer ate a light breakfast, the sun had chased the fog away, and she started fearfully toward The Crossroads. Sweaty hands gripping the steering wheel, she negotiated the hairpin curves at a crawl, holding her breath until she'd safely rounded each turn. She had calmed considerably when she reached Mountain Glen, and she felt as if she'd been given new strength. She'd heard that praying could chase away fear, and since she hadn't prayed for herself, was someone else praying for her safety on this torturous road? Autumn and Nathan or her parents?

School was in session when she arrived at The Crossroads, but Summer found Edna in her office. She gave Summer a key to the cabin.

"Go ahead and start settling in, but leave any heavy luggage until after school is over and the bigger boys can help you. I'm waiting for a telephone call, and I'll come along as soon as possible to give you any assistance you need. Do you remember the way to the cabin?''

''I'm sure I can find it,'' Summer answered.

Carrying two bags of groceries she'd purchased in Asheville, Summer located the path to the cabin. Determined to make the best of this situation, she hummed the tune of a popular song as she walked briskly toward her new home. Could she find contentment at The Crossroads as Bert and Spring had done?

She found no contentment in the cabin. The combination living room and kitchen was topsy-turvy. Boxes that had been on the table and sink counter when she'd been here before were scattered all over the floor. The upholstery and chairs were full of holes and tufts of padding littered the rooms. Summer advanced into the room slowly, wondering what vandals had been at work.

As she surveyed the room, a small head appeared in a hole in the couch and beady eyes peered at her. She started to run until she recognized the intruder as a squirrel. The animal scampered off the couch, ran to the fireplace and disappeared up the chimney.

Wondering how one small animal could have caused so much destruction, Summer was still standing thunderstruck in the middle of the room when Edna walked into the cabin.

''What's happened?'' she asked, alarmed.

''I scared a squirrel away from the couch and he ran up the chimney.''

''What a mess! I should have been checking the house, but we've been so shorthanded, I didn't think about it. The little critters must have chewed a hole in the screen over the chimney. This time of year they're looking everywhere for food.'' She dipped her hand into one of the holes on the couch and pulled out a handful of acorns. ''Apparently they intended to use the house for their storage bin. What about the rest of the house?''

''The door into the bedrooms is closed,'' Summer said as she opened the door to the hallway and glanced into the bedrooms. ''Seems okay in here.'' She looked helplessly at the damaged furniture. ''David will be here with Timmy and Nicole tomorrow.''

Edna shook her head. ''You do have a problem. A neighbor, Stonewall Blackburn, does handiwork for us, and I'll ask him to cover the chimney for you.''

She went to a closet near the front entrance and set out a broom, sweeper, mop and a bucket. ''This is probably all you'll need to tidy up the place. I'll send one of the older girls to help you this afternoon.'' Edna looked over the damaged upholstery. ''If you stuff this padding back in the holes, you can cover the furniture with blankets and get by all right.''

Summer had never been in a situation before when she had to get by. If something like this had happened in the Weaver household, they would have refurbished the whole place with new furniture. But you're not in the Weaver household anymore, she reminded herself. You're at a mission school.

Summer put the groceries in the cabinets and refrigerator, wondering if her bank account would stretch to buy a living room suite. If she let her parents know, they'd buy new furniture for the house, but she wouldn't impose on them more than she had to. She'd accepted this obligation, and she'd have to make out on her own.

She picked up the mop and looked at it with distaste. At home, they'd employed a housekeeper, and in New York, she'd used a cleaning service. She hardly knew where to begin. What had she gotten into?

Chapter Seven

Summer wanted to sit down and cry as she looked at the disordered cabin that was going to be her home for at least a year, but she wouldn't let the situation get her down. Besides, there wasn't a chair she'd sit on until she'd cleaned the place, and secondly, she'd made up her mind before she left New York that she was through with tears. She'd cried more in the last six weeks than she'd cried in her whole life. Clara had discouraged crying in her daughters, and she'd set an example for them. So no more crying!

Swearing and slang words were also forbidden to the Weaver daughters, so if she couldn't cry and she couldn't swear, what outlet did she have for her frustrations? There was nothing she could do but grin and bear it!

Summer walked back to her car to get a suitcase containing jeans and sweatshirts, noticing many squirrels scurrying around in the oak trees. It was useless to clean until the little creatures were barred from the cabin, but she returned to her new home to learn that Edna had moved quickly to alleviate that problem.

A lanky, black-bearded man, dressed in overalls and boots with a black hat pulled down over his long gray hair, sat on the steps. He appraised Summer with piercing, black eyes.

"Howdy! I'm Stonewall Blackburn. Miss Stollard said you had a fireplace problem, and she wants me to fix it."

"Thanks for coming right away, Mr. Blackburn. The squirrels have nearly ruined the living room. Can you find how they got into the house?"

Lazily, Stonewall unlimbered his long body and looked speculatively at the roof. "Won't be much of a job," he assured her. "I see where the varmints have pushed up the screen. Probably one of the chimney bricks fell and made a hole for the squirrels to get in. I'll have it fixed nice and tight in an hour or so."

"That will be great," Summer said. "I'll go ahead with my cleaning."

By the time Summer had spent an hour trying to push the stuffing back into the couch and the chair, her fingers were scratched from contact with the sharp springs, and her temper was frayed even more. She was going to buy a new living room suite! She didn't know much about being a missionary, but she was sure God didn't expect His servants to live in substandard housing if they didn't have to. Maybe she couldn't bring up her niece and nephew in the kind of surroundings she'd known as a child, but at least they'd have a couch where the springs didn't poke them when they sat down.

Summer brushed the rubbish off the table and cabinets onto the floor, and then wielding the broom vigorously, she swept all the debris into a dustpan to deposit in a waste container. While she worked, she heard hammering on the roof, so she assumed Mr. Blackburn was getting that job taken care of.

Before she finished washing off the cabinets and the tabletop, she heard a knock at the door, and a youthful voice said, "All right to come in?"

A girl stood in the doorway. "Miss Stollard said you needed some help. I'm Anita Bailey."

"I do need help, Anita. I'm Summer Weaver."

"Yeah, I know. I met you when you were here before."

Summer took another look at the girl. "Oh, yes, I remember. You were helping in the kitchen."

Anita surveyed the room. "Miss Stollard said things were in a mess, but they're not too bad."

"I've already swept, but the floor needs to be mopped. I'll get to that next and then I want to change the sheets and pillowcases. I'll have to do laundry, but I haven't seen a washer and dryer."

Anita wagged her head. "You'll have to use the community laundry at the girls' dorm. I can do the mopping if you want me to."

"I'd appreciate it, for if I'm to be ready when Mr. Brown comes with Timmy and Nicole tomorrow, I'll have to hurry." Eyeing the couch with distaste, she said, "I'm going to town this afternoon to replace the couch and chair, which I hope will be delivered tomorrow morning."

"I can help you patch up the furniture. That's the way we did at home."

"Thanks, but I'll try to buy something else."

Anita picked up the bucket and filled it with hot,

sudsy water and began mopping. She had large wistful brown eyes, straight black hair falling below her shoulders, a thin face and a twang to her voice.

Summer went into the bedrooms, removed the bed linens and put them in a laundry basket. She took fresh covers from the closet in the bathroom, and by the time Anita finished mopping, the bedrooms were habitable. Edna appeared at the door accompanied by two boys carrying Summer's luggage.

"This is all except what you have in the trunk. Where do you want to put it?" Edna asked.

"We'll stack the cartons in the bedroom, and I'll unpack when I can. First, I'll need to do something with their clothes. Do you have any suggestions?"

"A lot of used clothing is donated to the schools, so if there's anything you don't want to keep, we'll be glad to have them. Anything our students can't use, we sell at a yard sale once a year."

"I'll try to sort out everything tonight, and perhaps you can store them for me. I don't feel like giving their possessions away yet."

Indicating the boys who were bickering with Anita, Edna said, "Summer, these are two of the residents at The Crossroads." She indicated the closest boy. "This is Skipper Johnson. He came to us about six months ago."

Skipper flashed Summer a wide smile, and his dark eyes gleamed happily. He didn't seem to have a problem of any kind, and Summer wondered why he was at the school.

"Hi, Miss Summer. Hope you like it here."

The other boy, whom Edna introduced as Mayo Sinclair, was about Skipper's age, but where Skipper was a short, chunky kid, Mayo was thin and of medium height. His unruly blond hair fell over a high forehead and somber blue eyes concealed his thoughts.

"I'm glad to meet you," Summer said, "but I don't know much about boys. I don't have any brothers. Growing up, I considered that a blessing."

Anita wrung out the mop vigorously and laughed. "It *is* a blessing," she piped, eyeing the two boys saucily. "You'll find that out after you've been around these two for a while."

Skipper reached out and pulled vigorously on Anita's hair and she swung the mop at him.

"That's enough," Edna said in a quiet voice that carried authority. The scuffling ceased. "Summer, do you need help unloading the trunk of your car?"

"Yes, please. I have a computer in the trunk with most of my clothes piled around it."

"Wow! You got your own computer?" Skipper said.

"Yes. I brought some educational games for Timmy and Nicole."

"Teenagers like educational games, too," Skipper said, a hopeful gleam in his eye.

"We'll see. No promises yet," Summer said, already sensing the many needs of these teens, but hesitant to commit herself until she talked with David. They had to work as a team at The Crossroads.

After the boys left, Summer said to Edna, "I think my budget will stretch to buy a new sofa and chair. Is there a furniture store in Asheville that would have any bargains?"

"A few stores are always having sales."

"Then I'll drive into town this afternoon to see if I can find anything to be delivered tomorrow. I'd like to have the house in shape before David comes with the children.''

"It might upset Nicole and Timmy to have the furniture changed.''

"I hadn't considered that. But the sofa and chair are already changed. I'd think it would be more upsetting to find the furniture in shambles.''

"You may be right," Edna agreed, "but Timmy and Nicole will have a difficult adjustment to make when they return here without their parents. If you do buy new furniture, we'll take this to our workshop and see if we can redo it. We have an upholsterer who comes for short periods to teach his craft to our students.''

Summer turned to Anita. "Will you go to town with me?''

Anita turned quick, hopeful eyes toward Edna. "Am I allowed?''

Edna hesitated. "We have a closed campus here,'' she explained to Summer, and Anita turned away, "except for the children who live in Mountain Glen. Residents at The Crossroads leave only if they have a special permit to visit their family.''

"But there's some of us who don't have a family,'' Anita said.

Sympathy shone in Edna's eyes. "Bert often took the boys when he had supplies and equipment to buy, and I think this trip could be considered a similar situation. It's okay.''

"Thanks, Miss Stollard,'' Anita said.

"Let's leave right away, so we can be back before dark,'' Summer said. "I don't like mountain driving.''

Before they got to Asheville, Summer decided the

trip was beneficial in several ways, for Anita was a well of information. As she talked, Summer felt she couldn't have gotten a better orientation to the workings of The Crossroads.

"I was the first student to come to The Crossroads. I helped Bert and Spring finish painting the rooms and move in furniture. Anything you want to know, ask me. I know all about the place."

"Came from where and why are you at The Crossroads, Anita?"

Anita's expression changed from animation to bleakness. "It's kinda hard to talk about."

"Forget I asked. I don't want to distress you."

"Oh, it's all right. There wasn't anybody but me and my mom. We lived in Statesville, and when she died, I didn't have any place to go and nobody to turn to. I'd gone to Sunday school at a church near our apartment, and the pastor who preached Mom's funeral took me to stay with his wife until they found a place for me. They knew Miss Stollard, and they contacted her. They weren't ready for students, but she told them to bring me. Bert and Spring were good to me, but it still isn't home. I feel like a prisoner sometimes."

"Surely you have some relatives."

"Probably do, somewhere, but Mom was an only child, and her folks had died young. When I asked her about my father, she said I was better off not to know." She sighed. "You know, it makes me feel awful hopeless when I realize I'm all alone. I trusted the Browns to take care of me, and they're gone, too."

"You really aren't alone. Miss Stollard is fond of you, and I'm sure the other residents are, too."

"I don't get along with most of them."

To get Anita's mind off of her background, Summer asked, "What subjects do you like best in school? What would you like to do?"

"That's just it!" Anita said. "What hope do I have to make anything of myself? I don't have a dime of my own. The few things my mother owned were sold to pay her funeral expenses. She'd done domestic work, so she didn't have any insurance."

Summer knew she was ill-suited to advise Anita. How would Spring have encouraged the girl? If she succeeded at this work, she had to think like her sister would have done.

"I don't know much about this, Anita, but I'm sure there are grants available so you can go to college. Are you a senior?"

She nodded. "I'll get my high school diploma next spring."

"Have your grades been good enough for you to attend college?"

"Not bad," Anita admitted, "but I could have done better. There just didn't seem to be any reason to."

"There's always an incentive to make good grades. Since you're without parents, you'll have to take the initiative in making your own living. An advanced education will help you do that. So how about studying real hard this winter, and I'll look into grants that might pay your way through college."

"Okay," Anita agreed, but not enthusiastically.

Seeming to forget her own problems, Anita launched into a rundown of some of the other residents.

"Skipper Johnson is another one who could be a

good student, but he just doesn't care. His mother is still living, and she comes to see him every month, but Skipper had gotten out of hand. He was running with the wrong crowd, and she brought him to The Crossroads.''

They were on the outskirts of Asheville by this time, and Summer started looking for the furniture stores Edna had mentioned.

''And then there's Mayo Sinclair,'' Anita continued. ''His mother deserted him when he was a little boy. His father's a musician and out on tour most of the time. Mayo was wandering around the streets of Nashville, living in a mission at night, and the director of the mission arranged for him to come to The Crossroads. He likes it here, knowing he'll have three meals a day and a place to sleep. That guy can play almost any musical instrument—got the talent from his father, I reckon. There's an old banged-up piano in the chapel, and Mayo can make it talk! But he's not very good in books. Mr. Brown was just about to get through to these guys, so I don't know what will happen to them now.'' She favored Summer with a skeptical glance. ''Do you think the other Mr. Brown will be any good?''

''I'm sure he will,'' Summer answered, ''but you'll have to give both of us time. This kind of work is new to us.''

They tried several stores before finding furniture Summer could afford and that would be delivered to The Crossroads the next day. When they left the store, with her bank account badly depleted, and knowing there was little chance of having anything added to it, Summer reluctantly motioned to a nearby sandwich shop.

"Want to have a hamburger and fries before we go back?"

"I'd love it," Anita said, her eyes dancing with anticipation. "I get tired of the food at The Crossroads."

David and the children arrived the next evening soon after school dismissed for the day, and he blew the horn of the large van he was driving to alert everyone to their arrival. Timmy and Nicole jumped out of the van and scampered to the playground to greet their friends. Edna came from the school building.

"I've been praying for your safe arrival," Edna said, clasping his hand firmly.

"Is Summer at the cabin?"

"Yes, but I see her coming now. She must have heard you arrive."

David turned to greet Summer, held out his right arm and she ran into his embrace. Her eyes were glowing with pleasure, and there wasn't any doubt she was glad to see him. But why? Was she beginning to take a personal interest in him or was she just glad to see anyone she knew? He wanted to kiss her again, but he decided this wasn't the time or the place. She nestled content against his firm body for a few glorious moments, then she shook her head and drew away.

"Where are the kids?"

He motioned toward the playground. "Working off a lot of excess energy, I hope. I stopped often for them to exercise, but they kept pushing to come home." A tender expression brimmed his eyes as he smiled at her and took her hand. "As far as that goes, I was eager to get here, too."

Summer's eyes shifted quickly from the tenderness

in his gaze. "Isn't that Daddy's van?" she asked incredulously.

"Not anymore. It's ours now."

"Are you serious?"

"Look!" He pointed to the side of the van. Instead of the Weaver's Belgian Horse Farm sign that had been there the last time she'd seen the van, there was a new placard—The Crossroads, Mountain Glen, North Carolina.

Conscious of the crowd of students gathering around them, he released her hand reluctantly and said, "I'll tell you about it later."

Several of the older boys were surveying the eight-passenger van, exclaiming over its sleek chestnut finish, specially painted to match the Belgian horses at the Weaver farm. The van was only three years old, and it was a beautiful vehicle.

"Need any help, Mr. Brown?" Skipper asked.

"I don't believe so. I brought my things to The Crossroads before I left for Ohio, and the kids hadn't taken much with them. I believe Summer and I can handle everything. Nicole," he called, "will you and Timmy be all right while we unpack?"

Nicole, too busy playing to respond, waved a hand.

"I'll look after the children," Edna said.

"We've been riding several hours today, so they do need some exercise."

"Have you gotten along all right with them?" Summer asked as David handed her a couple of backpacks, took two suitcases and turned toward the cabin path.

"All right, I suppose," he said, "but it bothers me that they wouldn't talk about Spring and Bert. I'm worried about how they'll adjust now that they're at home without their parents.''

"I'm scared, David."

"It'll work out—don't worry."

"What's this about the van?"

"Your mother sent you a letter. I'll let you read it."

"Oh! Oh!"

They stepped into the cabin with the luggage, and David glanced around. "You've gotten everything looking great, but it seems different somehow."

Summer pointed to the sofa and chair. "New furniture," she said, and explained about the devastation she'd found in the cabin.

"That must have been an eye-opener!"

Summer nodded. "I was tempted to turn tail and run, and that isn't the only time, either."

"I've felt the same way, but we're both here, and we'll handle this assignment one way or another."

He took an envelope from his pocket, written on the gray stationery bearing the Weaver coat of arms that Clara had used for years. "Here's your letter."

"There's some tea in the refrigerator," Summer said, sitting on the new sofa. The message was short and she read it aloud.

"Dear Summer,

Regardless of their parents' request, it is *not* your and David's sole responsibility to take care of Nicole and Timothy. If you provide a stable home for them, the least we can do is help with the finances. I'm sure the school can use a van, and we'll be sending a substantial check each month for you and David to use for whatever you need. Over their protests, we occasionally helped Bert and Spring with necessities, and we don't expect any arguments from the two of you. What wealth we've accumulated will eventually pass to our children, and we can't see any reason to hoard up everything until we die when you need help now. So, please, don't be stubborn! We can't anticipate your necessities, so we're expecting you to let us know what you need.

Lovingly,
Mother and Daddy.''

Summer's lips trembled a little when she looked up at David. "What are we going to do?"

He arched his eyebrows. "I brought the van, didn't I? With a title made out in both our names."

"What'd you do with your car?"

"I'd already traded it for a secondhand Jeep, so I gave that to your father." He laughed. "It doesn't compare favorably with his other vehicles so he's probably gotten rid of it by now."

He sat beside her on the sofa. She tucked the sheet of paper into the envelope. "I argued with your parents about the van, and I agreed finally, but with a whole lot of misgiving. I've been independent for so long, it isn't easy for me to be on the receiving end."

"I know! I didn't realize how much I'm like Mother until she called it to my mind recently. It won't be as difficult for me to take from my parents as it will be for you, but I wonder if it's *right* for me to do so. I've gotten the notion that missionaries are supposed to sacrifice."

"As a child, I thought that missionaries were oddballs, who dressed in cheap clothing, lived from hand to mouth and enjoyed poverty. But I learned differently when missionaries came to speak at our church. They dressed in fashionable clothes, drove cars and were ordinary people like the rest of us.''

David's arm encircled Summer's shoulder, causing her heart to race, and she snuggled close to him. Her tenure at The Crossroads seemed so much simpler when David was around.

''Edna's example has caused me to wonder. She's been here for years, and from what I've observed, she cares nothing for what goes on away from these schools. She believes God will provide whatever she needs.''

''And He will,'' David agreed. ''I still have faith enough to believe that, but Edna doesn't have the same needs we have.''

Summer moved away from him and patted the sofa. ''Before I bought this sofa and chair, I decided that God wouldn't expect us to sit on ruined furniture. Perhaps I came up with that thought to excuse my own wants, for Edna made it plain that many people would be happy to have what I threw away. This change in my economic status has made me study my past lifestyle, and I don't always like what I see.''

''If you haven't already prepared a meal for this evening, let's eat at The Crossroads cafeteria.''

''Suits me,'' Summer said, ''but I don't want to make a habit of it. The children will eat at the school cafeteria at noon, I suppose, but they should have as ordinary a home life as possible. But another day's reprieve from domestic work will suit me. I haven't cooked for anyone except myself, and I don't know what children like to eat. I did buy a cookbook before I left New York, so that may help.''

"Let's go and collect the kids and see if they're ready for supper."

Biting her lip, Summer's hand whitened as she gripped the doorknob. She'd never dreaded anything as much as she did this meeting with her niece and nephew.

David sensed her uneasiness, and he gently pulled her into the circle of his arms. "Don't be nervous," he said. "It won't be that bad. The kids are lovable, and so are you, so you'll get along all right."

"The times I encountered them at the farm last month, I didn't have much to say to them. They both preferred Autumn to me. I could tell."

David tenderly massaged the tense muscles in her neck and shoulders. "But that was before they knew you were going to be their new mother."

"Mother! Don't even say the word! I doubt that I have any maternal instincts at all. Being a woman doesn't automatically make one a mother. Never in my life have I envisioned myself as a mother."

"Summer, you've agreed to do this, so stop having all these doubts. In the past few weeks, I've been reading the Bible and praying for the kind of fellowship with God that I used to have. I found a verse in the book of Isaiah that speaks to our situation. 'Strengthen the feeble hands, steady the knees that give way. Say to those with fearful hearts, Be strong, do not fear.' Although we think we're doing this for Bert and Spring, I believe we've undertaken this assignment for God, and if so, He's going to see us through it."

"I'd never thought of it that way."

"Do you have a Bible?" She shook her head against his shoulder. "Get one of Spring's Bibles and start reading it. The only way we can possibly succeed here is with God's guidance.''

He gave her another tight squeeze and released her. Cuffing her lightly on the shoulder, his eyes crinkled into a broad smile as he said, ''Straighten your shoulders and remember you're a Weaver.''

Chapter Eight

Timmy and Nicole sat on a bench in front of The Crossroads administration building with Edna between them. The kids smiled at David, but they ignored Summer.

"We'll eat in the cafeteria tonight," David said.

"Good idea," Edna answered. "I'll have Anita prepare extra trays. Let me know if there's anything I can do to help you get settled in."

"Let's go in the rest room and wash our hands before we eat," Summer said, and her words were slurred because her mouth was so dry.

"My hands ain't dirty," Timmy said sullenly.

"Oh, yes, they are," David said. "I'll go with you."

"I can help you, Nicole," Summer offered.

"I don't need help," Nicole stated and flounced off the bench.

A true Weaver, Summer thought, even though she had the brown hair and eyes and slender build of the

Browns. Timmy had inherited Spring's features—auburn hair and ocean-blue eyes.

When they came from the rest rooms, Timmy and Nicole hurried to sit with the students, who were glad to see them and made room for them at their tables. Edna stood near a table with seven adults, and she motioned for David and Summer to sit with them.

"This is a good opportunity for you to meet the staff with whom you'll be working." She turned to the people at the table. "David Brown and Summer Weaver have been appointed to replace their siblings. They've committed to our school for a year."

Curious but welcoming eyes were turned in their direction by the staff members, all of whom were senior citizens. Summer remembered Edna's comment that the teachers were volunteers. As Edna introduced the staff, Summer tried to associate the names and faces with their teaching responsibilities so she could remember them later.

David talked easily while they ate, but Summer spoke only when someone directed a remark toward her. Neither Timmy nor Nicole seemed to like her. How could she bear it if they continued to act this way?

Summer had hoped for David's support, but when dinner was over, he said, "I'll unpack some of my clothes and make my room livable. Everything is still in boxes and suitcases. If I finish in time, I may come over tonight. If not, I'll stop by in the morning. I've tried to explain to the kids why we're here, but I'm not sure they understand."

The Crossroads residents were busily clearing away the dinner trays and washing the tables, and Nicole and Timmy hovered near the door. Forcing a smile,

Summer went to them and said, "It's time for us to go home. You're probably anxious to see your dinosaurs, Timmy."

He shook his head, but they went outside with her and turned toward the path, their feet dragging. Summer wondered what troubled thoughts must be going through their heads. How could she take away the hurt they must feel?

"Did you enjoy the Belgian horses at Grandpa's?" she asked.

"I liked the fillies," Timmy said. "Grandpa said he might give me one when I get bigger."

"That would be a nice gift," Summer agreed. "Did you like the horses, too, Nicole?"

"Not particularly," she said in a grown-up manner. "I liked Aunt Autumn's baby best. She let me hold Lannie lots of times."

"He's got hair same color as mine," Timmy said.

When they came in sight of the cabin, Timmy and Nicole broke into a run, and Summer hurried to keep up with them. They raced up the steps, opened the door and stopped abruptly in the middle of the empty living room.

"Mommy," Timmy called, and he darted into the hallway. "You're here, ain't you? Mommy!" His blue eyes sparkled with tears when he ran back into the living area.

Summer knelt beside him and tried to take him into her arms, but he jerked away from her. "I want my Mommy and Daddy."

"Don't you remember the funerals at the farm, Timmy? Your parents aren't here anymore."

He shoved Summer, and she fell backward. Nicole ran to Timmy and took his hand.

"I told you they wouldn't be here, Timmy," she said, in a patient voice. "They went back to Bolivia, but they're coming back in a few months—maybe by Christmas."

"That isn't true," Summer said, earning her belligerent glances from both children.

Nicole looked around the room. "Where's our sofa and chair?" she demanded.

Summer put a tentative hand on Nicole's shoulder. "Squirrels broke into the cabin and chewed up the furniture. I had to replace them."

Timmy kicked the new chair. "I don't like it," he shouted. "That other chair is where Daddy and I watch television." He started crying and bolted down the hallway to his room.

"He wants to sit in the old chair," Nicole said.

Forcing a sickly smile, Summer answered, "Then he'll have to go to the storage room. The squirrels ruined the chair. He can't sit in it until it's repaired. I thought you'd be pleased with new furniture."

"Well, we're not! You've ruined our home."

Timmy came back into the room, carrying a blanket which he dropped on the floor, flipped on the television and laid down on the blanket. Nicole stepped in front of him and turned off the television.

"Hey. Stop that!" Timmy yelled.

"You know you're not supposed to watch television until you've washed. Get up off the floor and go take a shower. You stink."

Nicole jerked the blanket from under him, wadded it into a ball and pitched it on the sofa.

Timmy jumped up and started beating his sister on the back, and Summer watched in stunned silence. What was she supposed to do now?

She tried to separate the two children, but Nicole was hitting back, and Summer got a punch in her side. She didn't know that David had arrived until he shouted, "What's going on?"

The fighting stopped immediately when David stalked into the room. Summer backed away and leaned against the kitchen sink. David's eyes were angry. "What do you kids think you're doing?"

"Timmy was watching television before he took a bath. He knows better," Nicole said.

"She took my blanket," Timmy accused petulantly.

"He's nothing but a baby."

"That's enough!" David said. "Nicole, you know he can't take a shower by himself. Timmy, go to the bathroom. I'll be in to help you in a few minutes. Both of you have had a long day, and you're going to bed. Hike!"

Seeing how David had taken control, Summer knew she'd failed her first test. She ran outside, and in the dim light, she made her way to the bench overlooking the mountain vista, sat down and clenched her hands to stop the trembling. Why had she ever agreed to take on this responsibility? Timmy and Nicole needed someone who understood children. Someone to love them. Momentarily, Summer wondered if she loved anyone. She respected her parents, she admired her sisters, but love? She didn't know. If she didn't have any natural maternal instincts, perhaps she didn't have the capacity to love.

Summer shivered and wrapped her arms around her body. The lightweight shirt and slacks she'd worn all day were too thin now, but in her agitation, when she left the cabin, she hadn't thought about bringing a coat.

She was surrounded by darkness, and stars appeared in the sky—little white lights at first, but as they increased in number, the stars seemed to illuminate the distant hills.

She glanced back at the cabin. There was a light in the children's bedroom, so perhaps David was putting them to bed. She couldn't sit out here all night, but she dreaded going back to face David and the children.

She heard a step behind her, and sensing it was David, she didn't turn. He draped a blanket around her shoulders, then he sat beside her. Reaching for her hands, still clenched in her lap, he tenderly disentangled the tense fingers. He moved close to her and spread the blanket over both of them. Warmth from his body and the blanket soon enveloped Summer.

Things didn't seem quite so bad when David was beside her, but she said, "I knew I couldn't do it. I should never have come."

"This was a bad day for you and the kids. They'd gotten used to me, but you're still a stranger to them. When they walked in the cabin without their parents, it must have hit them for the first time that Spring and Bert weren't coming back."

"No, you're wrong. Timmy ran around the cabin calling for Spring. Nicole told him their parents had gone to Bolivia, but they'd be home in a few months."

David stared at her, speechless for a few minutes. "How are we going to convince them otherwise?"

"I have no idea. Maybe Edna will talk to them."

"Tomorrow will be better."

"I hope so. I don't see how it can be any worse. Are they in bed?"

"Yes, and I think they've settled down, but we can't stay out here long, in case they should start fighting again."

"Too bad you can't be around all the time."

"Under the circumstances, I can't stay here at night, but there is one solution. You and I could get married and all be one happy family."

Summer's heartbeat sped up at the suggestion, which surprised her, but she knew David was joking as he often did.

"I think we can manage better than that. I'll try it for a few weeks, and if it doesn't work out, maybe they can go back to Ohio until they adjust to their parents' death."

She stood up, and in the darkness, she didn't see the stupefied look on David's face. He was surprised at himself. What would he have done if she'd taken him up on his offer? He was getting along just fine alone, and with the two kids to look after and a school to supervise, he had about all the responsibility he wanted. He hadn't considered taking a wife since he'd had a crush on the girl next door when he was sixteen years old. Still, there was something different about his feelings for Summer. The past few weeks since they'd been together so much, he couldn't get her out of his mind. And coming from Ohio, he constantly caught himself speeding until he set the cruise control. He knew he wasn't that eager to arrive at The Crossroads and face his duties here. No, it was obvious, he was in a hurry to see Summer again.

"Let me check on the kids," he said, as they

walked up on the porch, "before I go back to the dorm."

"Please do," she said, and waited in the living room until he returned.

"They're sound asleep as far as I can tell, but I don't know much about kids, either."

"You knew enough to settle the fight and get them in bed. Thanks, David."

"Glad to be helpful," he said lightly. She looked so forlorn standing in the middle of the room, he hated to leave her, but he gave her a thumbs-up and left.

Moving quietly so she wouldn't waken the children, Summer changed into pajamas and slipped beneath the heavy blanket on the bed. It felt good to stretch out on the smooth sheets. Her body was tired, but her mind was still active, and she hesitated to turn out the light. Last night she'd kept the hall light on, but she wouldn't do that tonight, for Nicole and Timmy might be used to sleeping in the dark.

Although she'd acted nonchalant when David had made the comment about marriage, Summer wasn't as unaffected as she'd seemed. It surprised her to realize that the idea wasn't as disagreeable to her as it would have been a few months ago.

"That's only because we've *had* to be together to work out the terms of Bert and Spring's last requests." Summer told herself. "If it wasn't for that, I wouldn't need his company."

Summer picked up the Bible lying on the bedside table. Had Spring been in the habit of reading the Bible before she went to sleep at night? Would the Bible provide any answers for these unsettling thoughts about David?

She opened the Bible where a bookmark was placed. The page looked worn as if Spring or Bert had turned to it often. A few verses were underlined, and Summer read them aloud, "'On my bed I remember you; I think of you through the watches of the night. Because you are my help, I sing in the shadow of your wings. I stay close to you. Your right hand upholds me.'"

Could she depend on God to keep her through the night? It was an astonishing thought. Without knowing what it could really mean to trust God completely, Summer was able to put aside her fears of the future, and she turned out the light.

Chapter Nine

Summer bolted upright in bed, her heart pounding, her body shaking. A chill black silence surrounded her. Groggily, she threw back the blanket and swung her bare feet to the cold floor. What had awakened her?

"Mommy! Mommy!" Timmy screamed over and over, his voice echoing through the stillness of the cabin.

Summer turned on the light beside her bed, put on her robe and scurried across the hall. She had no idea what she could do to help Timmy, but she had to try. She paused on the threshold of his room. What if he rebuffed her again?

In the dim light from her bedroom, Summer saw Nicole sitting upright. Timmy writhed on his bed, still calling for his mother. Summer knelt beside him, and when she laid a gentle hand on his shoulder, he quieted.

"Timmy, wake up," she said. "You're having a bad dream."

"Mommy," he said again, but she thought he was still asleep.

"I'm Aunt Summer. Are you sick? What can I do to help?"

He started moaning, and Nicole said, "He has bad dreams lots of time when he's upset. Mommy always gave him a drink of water and got in bed with him until he settled down."

"Okay. I'll try that," Summer said. On wobbly legs, she brought a glass of water from the kitchen, sat on the bed and supported Timmy's back. A cold knot was where her stomach should have been.

"Here's a drink, Timmy." He took several deep swallows. She set the glass on the floor, moved Timmy over in the bed and lay beside him, her own body as stiff as a board. She tried to relax as she rubbed his back. Remembering a lullaby Clara had often sung to her when, as a child, she couldn't go to sleep, Summer sang quietly in her pleasing contralto voice, "Sleep on, my child, I'm always near, ready and waiting to calm your fears."

Timmy sighed and cuddled beside Summer. Did her voice sound enough like Spring's that he felt his mother was with him? Spring and Summer had been a lot alike, so perhaps that was the reason Spring had wanted her to be the children's guardian.

"Mommy used to sing that song to us," Nicole whispered. "Is he all right now?" Summer had forgotten about her.

"He seems to be sleeping. I'll stay here a while. You go back to sleep."

Nicole settled into bed, and Summer continued to hum the nursery rhyme until she lulled herself to sleep. The next thing she knew daylight was seeping into the small bedroom. She still lay on Timmy's bed, and a small hand was tapping her on the shoulder.

"I'm hungry," Timmy said. Did he remember what had happened last night? If not, he must wonder why she was in his bed.

"We'll see what we can do about that," she said, stretching and trying to get the kinks out of her back. Timmy's bed wasn't made for two people. "What do you eat for breakfast?"

"Cereal."

Summer had forgotten to remove her watch the night before, and she checked on the time. It was seven o'clock. Nicole turned over in bed when Summer started toward the hallway.

"What time do you go to school, Nicole?"

"After we eat breakfast."

"What about Timmy? Does he go to school?"

"He's in kindergarten. He's not old enough to be there, but Miss Edna lets him come because Daddy and Mommy had to work."

"Will you help Timmy wash his hands and get ready for breakfast? Do you want cereal, too?"

"Yeah."

Summer had bought a gallon of milk in Asheville, for she figured Spring's children would be fond of milk. The Weaver sisters had drunk lots of it, so she poured three glasses of milk and small glasses of apple juice. By the time Timmy and Nicole came to the kitchen, she'd placed several boxes of crunchy, sweetened cereal on the table, along with two bowls decorated with biblical characters.

"That's mine," Timmy said, seating himself at the table and grabbing the bowl featuring Noah and an ark full of animals. Nicole sat opposite him and took the other bowl.

"That's Mommy's chair," Nicole said, pointing to the chair at her left. Summer hesitated, not knowing whether to consider the statement an invitation to sit in Spring's chair or a warning not to. She perched on the chair, and when there was no protest, she poured a bowl of cereal for herself from a box of unsweetened wheat mix.

The two children hadn't started eating, and they stared at her intently. She glanced around the table. "Have I forgotten something?"

"We haven't said grace yet," Nicole said, and Summer's face flushed. Frantically trying to think of a way out of this predicament, she said, "Okay, which one of you wants to pray?"

"I do," Timmy said. He bowed his head as did Nicole, and in his childish voice said, "God is great, and God is good, and we thank Him for this food. Amen."

"Uncle David didn't listen to our prayers last night," Nicole said. "We can't forget tonight."

So that was another hurdle she had to face! She feared this was only the beginning of the marathon before her.

"Now that our Mommy has gone to Heaven, Uncle David says you're going to be our mother," Timmy said. His wide blue eyes were bright, reminding Summer of her sister.

Part of the time they must accept that their parents were dead!

"Did Uncle David tell you that's what your parents asked us to do?"

"Grandpa had already told us before he got to the farm," Nicole said.

"Then you know that your mother and daddy wanted to be sure you had someone to look after you if they should go to Heaven before you were old enough to take care of yourselves."

The kids nodded, their eyes serious.

"I'm going to be honest with you. I don't know anything about taking care of kids. Spring was a good mother because she'd had six years of practice, but you'll have to be patient with me. If I make mistakes, I hope you'll forgive me and let me try over."

"We'll help you," Timmy promised solemnly.

She motioned to the sofa. "When I came here a few days ago, the squirrels had chewed holes in the sofa and chair and the padding was scattered around the floor. I thought I was doing you a favor to buy new furniture, but if you're that unhappy about it, we can bring the old things back in."

Timmy left the table and climbed up into the chair. He wiggled around as if trying it on for size.

"It's okay," he said.

"Nicole?"

"We were sad last night," she answered. "You can keep the furniture."

"And there are lots of other things I don't know. Do you need help to put your clothes on? What time do you get up in the morning? What time do you go to bed? Do you come home for lunch, or do you eat at school?"

"I can dress myself," Nicole said, reeling off the answers one by one, "except maybe buttons in the back and help with my hair. Timmy needs help taking a shower and cleaning his teeth, and he still has trouble getting on his shoes and socks. He'll wear dirty clothes if you don't watch him. Uncle David dressed him in the motel yesterday morning. We get up about seven and go to bed at nine o'clock.''

"Sometimes we got to stay up later than that," Timmy protested.

"Not very often."

"We eat lunch at school," Timmy contributed.

"That's enough for me to remember right now," Summer said.

"Are you and Uncle David married?" Timmy asked.

"No," Summer answered, flustered. "What made you think that?"

"If you're going to be our mother, and he's our daddy, we just thought it ought to be that way," Nicole said.

"We're not supposed to take the place of your parents. We're still your aunt and uncle like always."

"Are you gonna get married?" Timmy persisted.

"We haven't talked about it," Summer answered, wondering why she didn't make an outright denial.

"What are we gonna call you?" Nicole asked.

"What's wrong with Aunt Summer?"

"The words are hard to say together," Timmy said.

"Auntie might be all right," Nicole said, her lips pursed, as if it were a weighty decision.

"That's fine with me. Right now, you need to get ready for school."

Supervising the children as they prepared for school was a revelation to Summer. She'd never been allowed to decide what she would wear until she'd started junior high school, but Nicole insisted that she choose her own garments. That wasn't much of a decision, for the school code provided that girls should wear a dark skirt and a white blouse. While Nicole dressed, Summer monitored Timmy cleaning his teeth. He ran into the bedroom, and when Summer got there, he'd stripped off his pajamas and stood naked waiting for her to help him dress. She gasped and started to reprimand him, but she quickly realized neither he nor Nicole thought anything about his natural state.

Swallowing her confusion, she turned to the three-drawer chest at the foot of his bed. Without looking at Timmy, she handed him a pair of shorts and a T-shirt, hoping he'd put them on by himself. When she finally turned with a pair of dark-blue trousers and a white shirt in her hands, Timmy had put on his underwear, but he had the T-shirt on backward. She removed it and pulled it over his head in the proper position.

Getting his tennis shoes on was no easy task, but the pair she chose closed with Velcro strips, which sped up the chore.

"I can't get my hair fixed right," Nicole complained, and Summer reached for the brush. "I want it brushed high on my head and this barrette put on it."

That wasn't hard for Summer because Nicole's hair was thick and manageable. She'd often helped Spring fix her hair in this fashion when they were teenagers, and it felt right to be performing the same service for Spring's daughter.

Summer was startled when David's voice sounded at the bedroom door. "Looks like everyone is about ready for school."

"I'm not sure," Summer said, looking up at him,

laughing. "I'd like a second opinion, if you don't mind."

"Hi, Uncle David," Timmy said, and rushed to his uncle, who swung him up into his arms.

"Hi, buddy. Looks like you're ready to be the star pupil in kindergarten today."

Summer snapped the barrette over Nicole's soft hair. "Does that feel all right?" she asked anxiously.

Nicole peered in the little mirror by the side of her bed. "Okay, I guess, but Mommy used to fasten it higher."

"I'll remember next time," Summer said, with a resigned look at David. He reached into the hall closet and handed out two coats. "You'll need to bundle up this morning," he said. "It's frosty outside."

"Grandma Weaver gave us these coats before we left the farm," Nicole told Summer.

"Do you walk to school alone or should I go with you?"

"We go by ourselves. Won't nobody hurt us up here," Nicole said. "C'mon, Timmy." She grabbed her brother's hand and hustled him out of the house.

"Whew!" Summer said when the door slammed behind the children. She dropped heavily on the new chair.

"Had a hard morning?" David asked sympathetically as he prepared the coffeemaker.

"It's probably a normal morning in a house with two kids, but I'm not used to such turmoil. For the time being, they seemed to have accepted me, so that's one advantage."

She leaned back in the chair and closed her eyes, savoring the rich aroma of coffee as the water dripped into the carafe. Summer was still dressed in her pajamas with a pink terry robe wrapped around her, but David's interested eye noted that even in nightclothes, she looked like a fashion model. She didn't stir until he tapped her on the shoulder.

"Drink this coffee. It'll perk you up."

She cuddled the coffee mug in both hands and sniffed the pungent aroma.

"Thanks. If you're hungry, there's a package of rolls in the refrigerator. I ate cereal with the kids."

"I took the cafeteria breakfast. It's not bad. Edna wants to meet with us this morning to organize our schedules and tell us what duties we have. Can you be ready in an hour?" he asked.

Summer glanced down at her garments and colored slightly. She'd forgotten that she still had on her robe, no makeup, and she hadn't combed her hair.

"Sorry I'm not more presentable, but I didn't get much sleep last night, and I overslept," she said apologetically and explained to him about Timmy's nightmare. "I'll straighten the house, and then it won't take long to shower and dress."

"If you want to take the bedrooms, I'll clear away the breakfast things and wash the dishes."

"Deal!" she said with a laugh.

She heard him whistling while she made the beds and put away the kids' nightclothes.

Summer thought of his comment the night before that they should get married. Was he serious about it? Would it be like this if they were married, sharing the responsibility of the house and taking care of the children?

If they were married! Summer was straightening the sheets on her bed, and she stopped abruptly. She could hear running water in the sink and David rattling the dishes as he cleared the table. Her whole outlook on life and many of her attitudes had changed the past few weeks. How much did David have to do with the change in her?

She'd never seriously contemplated marriage. Marriage meant losing your personal freedom by sharing it with another. She remembered the minister's reference to this fact during Autumn's wedding. He'd said, "You're no longer one person, you're now joined to each other," and Autumn and Nathan had lit a unity candle indicating that they'd become one. As she fluffed the pillows and arranged the comforter, Summer acknowledged that marriage also meant an intimate relationship. Her mind shied away from that possibility, but she did look at David in a different light when they walked along the path to the school compound.

Their footsteps crackled on the frosty grass, and their breath was visible. The sun's rays filtered slowly into the mountain valley and the air was still cold. Summer zipped her jacket.

"Are winters cold here? Do they have much snow?"

"I imagine so, but Edna will be able to answer your questions. We're to meet her in The Crossroads' office."

The administration building housed not only the offices, but the classrooms and cafeteria, and they heard the hum of student voices as they entered the building. Edna met them at the front door.

"You can see the schoolrooms when classes aren't in session, but the teachers' lounge and the administrative offices are down this way."

She pointed out a small room with several easy

chairs and a long table with straight chairs around it. One wall was lined with bookshelves. An ancient copier and one computer station was located near the door. "The teachers come here for their preparation time," Edna explained.

Next were two connecting offices, and Edna led the way into the largest room. "Bert used this office, and Spring did the secretarial work in the other room, but you can divide duties to suit yourselves."

She motioned David to the chair behind the desk, and as he sat there, he was overwhelmed with the loss of his brother. Perhaps Edna and Summer sensed his emotion for they sat opposite him and didn't speak. David stared at the stacks of unopened mail on the desk. A flash of loneliness overcame him and he closed his eyes. He felt so inadequate sitting in his brother's chair.

"Will you explain what we're expected to do?" Summer asked, giving David time to compose himself.

"It's a big job. You'll be responsible for handling the funds that come to the school and allocating them to cover the needs. There's never enough money. Fund-raising is also a part of the job. That's what Bert and Spring were doing when the accident happened. It's necessary for you to occasionally visit the churches that donate to the work and tell them what's going on."

"I'm not at ease speaking publicly, but David could do that, I'm sure."

"With your experience in business administration, Summer, perhaps you can take over the finances," David suggested in a strained voice.

"I'm sure I can."

"You must plan the curriculum with the teaching staff," Edna explained.

"And that's where I'll be lost," Summer said.

David shrugged his shoulders. "Same with me. I know nothing about the current educational system."

"You can rely on the teachers for advice until you learn. Of course, as supervisor of both schools, I'm available for consultation at any time. I'd suggest that each of you visit the classes on a regular basis for a few weeks. You'll learn more about the curriculum that way than my telling you."

The rest of the morning, David and Summer sifted through the accumulation of mail and started organizing the two offices to suit their own temperaments. When Summer looked over the financial records, she decided that Bert was a better missionary than he was an accountant, and she knew she'd have to start a whole new system. The ancient computer in the office was of little use, and while she'd intended to keep her personal computer in the house for the children, it could be put to better use in the office.

They ate lunch with the staff and students, and before they went back to the office, David said, "Let's walk down to the lake. I'm not used to being cooped up inside, and I could use some fresh air."

They sat on a bench overlooking the lake, silently watching a flock of ducks searching for food. The mountains were more colorful than they'd been during their first visit, for frost was steadily marching the colored leaves down the slopes. The air was fresh and invigorating. A jet stream slashed across the blue of the sky and a faint sound of the plane reached them, but otherwise, there was no sound except that of nature.

"This is a peaceful place," Summer said. "I'm beginning to have a slight inkling of why my sister wanted to live here. In New York, my windows were always closed to keep out the sound of traffic, but here I like to hear the blending of insects' songs."

David nodded his agreement, but his face was solemn. Obviously, the scenery wasn't on his mind.

"It's been a sad morning for me to be handling my brother's possessions, knowing I'll never see him again. There's a plaque on Bert's desk that quotes the words of Solomon. 'Generations come and generations go, but the earth remains forever.' These mountains haven't changed much since the Creation, and they'll still look the same thousands of years from now. When I considered how short life is, I asked myself why I hesitated about giving up a lucrative job to carry on the work our loved ones started."

"And I've been thinking about how nearly this work stopped because there was no money to carry on. If money hadn't been an issue, I'm sure the mission board could have found an administrator."

"The finances are bad, huh?"

"The school exists from month to month."

"At first, we'll have to go slowly. I couldn't sleep last night, either—fretting because I'd let myself wander so far from my Lord until I can't depend on Him for daily guidance. But I believe, if it's God's will, we'll succeed at The Crossroads. Bert and Spring started the work, but it's up to us to carry it on, until someone else takes the torch from us."

"So, just like Bert and Spring, we're stepping out on faith."

David rubbed his chin thoughtfully. "I remember from my Bible-reading days that in the New Testament, Paul the apostle said, 'I planted the seed, Apollos watered it, but God made it grow. So neither he who plants nor he who waters is anything, but only God, who makes things grow.' That may be the case here at The Crossroads.''

"You mean that Spring and Bert were the ones to plant the seed by establishing the school, you and I are to water it by placing the school on a secure foundation, but that God actually provides the growth?''

"That's the way I've figured it out.''

"That's a big responsibility, but it does give some meaning to why we're here.''

David shook his head and blinked his eyes as if to rid himself of such serious thoughts.

"Now why should I be so gloomy, when I'm sitting here in this beautiful glade beside a pretty lady!'' He put his arm around Summer's shoulders and a grin spread over his features. "You are pretty, Summer. Did anyone ever tell you that?''

Summer flushed slightly. "Not that I ever remember. Don't forget, I lived with a *real* beauty in the family. It's hard to measure up to Autumn.''

His fingers tightened on the soft flesh of her shoulder. "You underestimate yourself. I'd trade Autumn for you any day.''

"I'm sure her husband would be pleased to know that.''

"I'm serious. I like your short, straight hair, that's golden-bronze rather than auburn.'' His hand tenderly smoothed her hair as he spoke. "You're petite, you have dainty features, and skin the shade of a pale-pink rose.''

Her skin wasn't pink now, for Summer felt a rush

of blood to her face. "Oh, stop it, David! You're embarrassing me."

He laughed lowly, a provocative sound that sent her pulses racing. He turned her face to his and brushed her lips with his as he said softly, "This assignment at The Crossroads may not be so bad, after all. I'm having thoughts now that I've never had before. I like you, Summer, I like you a lot."

His lips gently covered her mouth, and for a few moments she surrendered to the floating sensation of being held close in David's arms. Then she pushed him away.

"David, you must stop kissing me! We have to remember why we're here—to operate a school for thirty teenagers and take care of two orphaned children. Any personal involvement between us will hamper what we came here to do. Promise you won't kiss me again."

"I won't make such a promise. I didn't intend to kiss you today, but I just get carried away when I realize how fascinating you are. Who's to know when it might happen again?"

With a slight grimace, she said, "Then I'll stop being fascinating." She stood up. "We should go back to work. I need to figure out how to operate a school on half the money Daddy spends to take care of his horses."

"I suppose you're right," he said. "I'll try to suppress my impulses."

Chapter Ten

Summer went back to the office and spent a couple of hours formulating a schedule for paying bills and making reports to the mission board. If they didn't run into any emergencies, they could keep to the budget. Her life had surely taken a different turn in the past few weeks! There was a vast difference between handling the finances of a prestigious New York bank and trying to balance books in a North Carolina mission school!

David had spent the afternoon in the adjoining room sorting through the mail that had accumulated since Bert had left the office. When Summer entered, he was tinkering with an electric typewriter, trying to get it to work.

"David, would you like to come to the cabin every evening and have dinner with the children and me? Otherwise, you'll have very little time with them."

His eyebrows arched provocatively. "You're not expecting a repeat of last night's actions, are you?"

"I didn't mean that at all." She turned abruptly toward her office. "Forget I mentioned it."

David was out of the chair with one swift movement and caught her arm. "Hey! I was joking. I'd love to come. I thought of suggesting it, but hated to invite myself."

Still annoyed at him, she said tersely, "You have as much right to that cabin as I do. I was just suggesting a way for you to have some time with the kids. Do what you want to."

"I'll be there. The kids need all the security we can give them. And please learn not to take offense when I joke with you. You need to loosen up a little, laugh and enjoy yourself."

"So I've been told before." She picked up her jacket and walked out of the office.

He watched her departure, irritated at himself. Why couldn't he watch his tongue?

Summer was annoyed with herself as she walked to the cabin. Why had she been so short-tempered with David? She wasn't that way with anyone else, but she was frightened because she was getting so fond of David. She still wanted to go back to New York and her career in a year's time, and she had to concentrate on that. An interest in David would interfere with that decision.

When the kids came home an hour later, David was with them, and Summer wondered if he'd arranged that deliberately to avoid being alone with her and her temper. Timmy ran into the house, dropped his book bag on the floor and turned on the television. Nicole threw her jacket on the sofa and sat beside her brother on the floor. Summer assumed this was their normal procedure as soon as they got home from

school, but her orderly instincts rebelled. She didn't
say anything, but she picked up the jacket and book
bag and took them to the children's bedroom. David
was setting the table when she returned, and she
didn't appreciate his amused expression when he
looked at her.

"What's for supper?" he asked.

"Broccoli and cheese casserole," she answered
shortly.

"Yuk!" Timmy said, his mind diverted momentarily from the television.

Summer paused in her task of preparing a salad. "I
take it you don't agree with my choice," she said.

"They feed us broccoli and cheese two or three
days a week at school. Mommy never fixed it at
home," Nicole said.

"Summer's casserole will taste better than what
you get at school." David came to her defense.
"What do you usually eat for supper?"

"Pizza, spaghetti, french fries and stuff like that,"
Timmy said.

"Now, Timmy, you know Mommy made us eat a
lot of vegetables and fruit," Nicole corrected him.

"I saw a frozen pizza in the freezer. How about
having that?" David asked Summer, and grinned
when he added, "I don't like broccoli, either."

Without answering, she took the pizza from the
freezer and prepared it for the oven. "I hope none of
you object to green salad."

"As long as you don't put any onions in mine,"
Nicole said.

"At home, we didn't question Mother's decisions
and ate what was put on the table," Summer commented quietly.

"Parents are more lenient with their kids now," David said.

When they were seated at the table, Nicole said the blessing, and Summer insisted that each child try a portion of the casserole. She plopped a spoonful on David's plate, too. "It won't hurt you to eat broccoli."

He obediently ate the food, and Nicole and Timmy followed his example. Summer was sure his presence in the cabin would help a lot with discipline. And remembering her pleasure in David's occasional caresses, she wondered if she'd wanted him around for more than one reason.

They were still at the table when a knock sounded at the door and a half-dozen Crossroads residents tramped in. "We came to watch television when Mr. and Mrs. Brown lived here," Skipper Johnson said. "Is that okay with you?"

"Sure, come in," David said. "You'll have to compromise with the kids on the channel you watch."

"No problem," Anita Bailey said. "Only one channel comes in up here. We watch the game shows for an hour. Mr. Brown thought they were educational for us."

Summer watched helplessly as the teens settled on the couch and on the kitchen chairs. The already small quarters seemed to shrink even more. She turned her back and gripped the edge of the sink.

David noticed her dismay, and he said quietly, "I'm sorry. I shouldn't have given the okay without consulting you."

"It's all right. But the house was already crowded with the four of us, and now I learn there'll be several more every night." She lifted her hand to her mouth and chewed on a long, pink fingernail. "I never understood what claustrophobia was until this moment."

He started clearing dishes off the table. "Go to your bedroom or out for a walk. I'll be here."

She shook her head. "I can't spend a year walking away from my problems. I'll have to learn to live with them."

During the rest of the week, Summer and her new family settled into a manageable routine starting with breakfast as soon as the children got up. They left for school between eight and half past eight, after which she straightened the house, showered and dressed for the day. She was in the office by nine o'clock, where David had already been working for an hour.

On the second morning, Nicole and Timmy lingered at the breakfast table, and Summer finally prompted, "Don't you think you should be going to school?"

"Not until after morning devotions," Nicole said. "Mommy read to us from the Bible and the devotional book before we left the table. We forgot yesterday."

Summer looked around wildly. If she was poorly equipped to provide food for these kids, how much less suitable was she to take over their spiritual training. *God, what am I going to do?* More and more she was turning to God in her extremity. Who else could help her?

"I haven't seen a devotional book," she said, masking her uneasiness.

"Mommy kept it in that basket on top of the 'frigerator," Timmy said.

Summer rose like a robot and reached for the basket which held a Bible and a small booklet, titled *Devotions for the Growing Family*. She saw at a glance that there was a page for each day of the year, and a bookmark was placed on the day that Bert and Spring had left their home. She hurriedly turned to the devotional for the present date.

The suggested Bible reading for the day was Luke 2:40, which presented another quandary. She was ashamed to ask Nicole to find the place for her, although she figured the child knew more about the Bible than she did. She noted the tabs on the pages, and scanning them quickly, she saw the one that marked Luke. Feeling as if her temperature had reached the boiling point, she flipped the pages to the second chapter. She read the designated verse.

"'And the child grew and became strong. He was filled with wisdom, and the grace of God was upon Him.'"

From the booklet, she read the thought for the day, "Parents are expected to guide and monitor a child's growth, insuring that the child grows up spiritually, as well as physically. A child should receive an adequate education, which includes learning the teachings of the Bible at an early age. Children are expected to love their mother and father, and parents should love their children. Love is the key to a happy home life."

Summer closed the Bible around the booklet, determined that she'd get more acquainted with the Bible before the next morning. Timmy and Nicole joined hands and stretched their free hands to Summer. She took the hands as the children waited expectantly.

"Mommy always prayed," Timmy said and bowed his head.

Cold sweat broke out on Summer, and she thought she was going to faint, but she cried out in her distress, "Oh, God!" She bowed her head and struggled for words. "Oh, God, help us today. Protect Timmy and Nicole at school and help them to learn their lessons. Amen."

The children squeezed her hands and jumped down from their chairs. They hustled into the bedroom, came back with their coats and book bags and stood expectantly before her.

She forced a smile. "Now what am I to do?"

"Mommy hugged and kissed us and told us she loved us before we went to school," Timmy said.

Tears welled up in Summer's eyes, and she knelt by the children and pulled them both into a tight embrace. "I love both of you," she mumbled over the lump in her throat. She released the kids and kissed them on the foreheads.

"Bye," Nicole said. Long after the children left the house, Summer sat at the table, her head in her hands.

While Nicole and Timmy seemed to be adjusting to the situation without their parents, Summer noticed that they were moody a lot of the time. They seldom opposed her instructions, but they bickered a lot between themselves. She and David agreed that they must spend some quality time with the children, so on the third Saturday, they took Nicole and Timmy into Asheville where they had lunch together, attended a movie and bought groceries. Summer believed that the kids might be more receptive to the foods she prepared if they helped buy the ingredients.

The kids were so excited over the outing that they temporarily forgot their parents' absence. All of them wanted to make the trip to town a weekly ritual.

When they returned from Asheville, Edna hailed them from the steps of the elementary school with news about the next day's worship plans.

Sunday was expected to be a day of rest and worship at The Crossroads. Edna conducted worship services in the auditorium at the elementary school. Bert had directed worship for The Crossroads residents in a small chapel located in a wooded area behind the dormitories. After his death, Edna had combined the two services at the elementary school.

"Since you've stated that you aren't spiritually experienced to lead the worship service, the mission board has arranged for a seminary student, Curtis Nibert, to come here for a year as the resident pastor. He will go to the seminary two days each week for classes, but the rest of the time, he can be on the field. Curtis was a short-term volunteer at the elementary school a couple of years ago, and he impressed me then. I think you'll like working with him. He'll be here in the morning."

"That's a relief off my mind," David said. "Several of the boys have mentioned the chapel services, acting as if they expected me to start them. The teenagers think they're too old to worship with the little ones."

The chapel was an unpretentious log building with a crude wooden cross nailed over the front door. The building had benches for fifty worshipers, and since attendance at Sunday chapel services was compulsory for the residents, the room was almost full when Summer arrived with Nicole and Timmy. Most of the staff members were present, too. David had saved a seat for their family near the front of the room. Mornings in the mountains were cold, but heat was provided by a small stove in the middle of the room, which Stonewall Blackburn was filling with small chunks of wood.

Edna was on hand to introduce Curtis, and Summer felt drawn to him immediately. A thin man in his midtwenties, he stood tall and erect. His almost white, blond hair gave Curtis the appearance of being prematurely gray. His blue eyes were eager, bright and full of laughter.

Mayo Sinclair was running through chords on a studio piano that was out of tune, and Summer thought of the grand piano at the Weaver home that was seldom used. All three Weaver daughters had taken piano lessons. Spring had become proficient on the instrument, but after she left home, the piano was seldom played. Mayo had a touch that made the piano sound as if it were talking.

David leaned across the two kids and whispered, "Mayo's father is a bluegrass musician."

Flashing the words on a screen from an overhead projector, Curtis led the group in singing several gospel choruses and David joined in a pleasing tenor voice. Summer didn't know the songs, and she had difficulty following, so she stopped trying. Curtis's message was brief, and although it was slanted mostly toward the students, Summer paid close attention to his words. Every day it seemed as if she encountered a new situation where she needed spiritual enlightenment in dealing with Timmy and Nicole.

The sun had chased the fog away by the end of the worship service, and they went outside to a warm, balmy October day and the pleasant scent of a mixture of pine and drying leaves. Deeply inhaling the fragrant air, David said to Summer, "Let's take the kids on a hike into the national forest this afternoon. There are several good trails, and we need to take advantage of the nice weather."

"I'm not an outdoors person," Summer said, "but if I'm going to live here, I'll have to be, I suppose. Why don't we take a picnic lunch?"

"That's a great idea. Let's ask the kids."

Nicole and Timmy enthusiastically agreed. Summer changed into jeans and a sweatshirt when she got home and laid out jeans and a shirt for Timmy. She searched the cabinets and refrigerator for picnic fixings.

"What do you kids want to eat? We could take cheese cubes, apples and cookies. Or we can make sandwiches out of the lunch meat we bought yesterday. There's a two-liter bottle of cola already cold in the fridge."

They preferred peanut-butter-and-jelly sandwiches, which she made hurriedly and packed them, some apples and a bag of cookies into a backpack she'd found among Bert's possessions. They were waiting on the porch for David when he arrived wearing jeans and a colorful plaid sweater. Summer hadn't seen him dressed so casually since that day over two years ago when they'd gone to the amusement park in Ohio.

David strapped the backpack over his shoulders and handed Summer a book he carried. "I found this in the office. It's a field guide to eastern trees. We might as well try to identify the trees in the forest while we walk.''

''I want to eat first,'' Timmy said. ''I'm hungry.''

''You're always hungry,'' Nicole said in disgust. ''You're going to get as fat as a pig if you don't watch out.''

''Will not,'' Timmy said belligerently, giving his sister a shove.

''Will, too.''

David lifted his eyebrows, and Summer wondered how peaceful this outing was going to be.

''Perfectly normal behavior between brother and sister,'' he murmured for Summer's ears alone. ''I had two sisters and they can be trying.''

''I had two sisters also, but Mother didn't allow us to quarrel.''

''I'll ignore it for a while,'' David said. ''Hopefully, they'll get tired of fussing in a few minutes and turn to something else.''

''There goes a deer,'' Timmy shouted and ran down the trail, but he couldn't match the speed of the leaping animal. When they came upon a terrapin, he said, ''I'm going to take it home and put it in a cage in my room.''

''No,'' Summer said. ''I don't want it in the house.''

''Aw, it won't hurt nothing.''

''He's right, you know,'' David said.

''No! After having the cabin riddled by squirrels, I won't have animals inside.''

''Mommy wouldn't care if I have it,'' Timmy shouted, stomping his feet.

The obvious answer was that his mother wasn't in charge of the house now, but Summer couldn't say that to him. She shook her head, and Timmy kicked a rock and ran ahead of them. Summer felt as if Nicole and David both thought she was being unreasonable because they stopped talking as they walked along the trail. When they stopped for lunch, Timmy couldn't be found, and it took David a quarter of an hour before he found where the child had hidden. After that altercation, no one seemed to have an appetite, and they nibbled silently on their food.

David eventually started identifying some of the trees they saw, and the kids would talk to him, but they said nothing to Summer. She wasn't in the mood to talk, either. When they returned to the cabin, she prepared spaghetti for their evening meal as a peace offering, for both children were fond of spaghetti. Still they didn't relent in their cool attitude toward Summer, and she was so tired that she didn't really care. As soon as David left, she sent Timmy and Nicole to bed, and she took a shower and got into bed, too.

She slept listlessly, once again depressed, wondering if she would ever be capable of dealing with two children. Mothers learned gradually how to raise their offspring. She hadn't had any on-the-job training. Suddenly she'd been handed two children, and she was expected to know how to handle them as if she were a pro. It was an impossible task.

When she entered the kitchen the next morning, the first thing she saw was a terrapin crawling across the floor. So Timmy had brought the creature in even when she'd told him not to! Had David known about it? Summer didn't want to touch the animal, but she wouldn't have it in the house. Taking a pot holder, she lifted the terrapin, annoyed that the varmint hissed at her before withdrawing into its shell. She carried it out to the edge of the forest and left it there.

Chapter Eleven

Annoyed at her own attitude as much as she was at David, Summer couldn't bring herself to talk when she went to the office, answering David with as few words as possible.

Finally, he said, "Why are you still angry?"

"I resented being treated like a pariah yesterday because I think wild creatures should be kept out in the woods. You and the kids talked, but left me out of the conversation, so I knew you were angry at me. You should support me in a few rules instead of making my task more difficult."

David's eyes narrowed. "I tried to talk to you, but you gave me some pretty short answers."

"Did you know Timmy brought that terrapin home with him?" she accused.

"No, I didn't."

"Well, he did, and it was crawling around in the kitchen when I got up this morning."

"What did you do with it?"

"Put it outside where it belongs. I don't expect you

to understand my way of life, but I've always been used to a neat, well-ordered home, which incidentally, I never cleaned myself. I'm not above working with my hands, and I'm trying to keep the cabin in some order. I can make allowances for the children's lax habits, but it's too much to expect me to operate a menagerie in the house. David, you can help me with this if you will. Whether you agree with me or not, I expect you to support my decisions.''

Before his irresistible grin, she found her irritation melting away, but she didn't relax her stern expression.

He gave her a playful mock salute. ''Consider it done. I'll have a man-to-man talk with Mr. Timothy. No more varmints in the house.''

True to his word when David came for the evening meal, he said, ''Where is Timmy? I'll have a talk with him.''

Summer grinned slightly. ''He's in the bedroom— he's been looking all over the cabin for the terrapin, but he hasn't asked me any questions.''

''Timmy, come here,'' David called.

Timmy walked slowly into the room.

''Why did you bring the terrapin home when your aunt told you not to?''

Timmy's lower lip drooped into a pout. '''Cause I wanted to.''

''That's not reason enough. Summer's trying to make a good home for you here, and she's not making many rules. But when she does, I expect you to do what she says.''

Timmy argued with David for a few minutes, but he finally said he was sorry for disobeying Summer, and she hoped that was the end of his rebellion. When she said this to David, he laughed.

"Don't count on it. Boys can be ornery. I know by experience."

Then while they were eating, Nicole said, "If we can't have a turtle for a pet, how about a dog?"

David tried to suppress his amusement, but at the confused expression on Summer's face, he burst out laughing.

"It's your call," he said to her.

"I'll have to take a rain check on that one," she said, amused in spite of herself.

"Don't you like dogs, Auntie?" Timmy asked.

"I like dogs. We had a dog on the farm when I was a child. He was Autumn's dog, but he didn't stay in the house. Let me see how I get along raising you two kids before I agree to having a dog. For that matter, I don't dislike terrapins, but they're not house pets."

Edna, David and Summer held semimonthly staff meetings to discuss plans and problems for the two schools and to correlate the activities. Curtis Nibert often sat in on the meetings. At twenty-five, Curtis was slender, but not tall, and in her few conversations with him, Summer had been amazed at his spiritual and emotional maturity. Still, his blue eyes gleamed with a boyish smile, his long blond hair was tied back in a ponytail and his casual dress attested to his youth.

When they gathered in David's office for the mid-November meeting, David asked, "What about Christmas arrangements? How long is the vacation period?"

"We have a two-week break, and several of the

children go home,'' Edna said. "The house parents stay in the dorm, so you and Summer can leave if you want to.''

"I wasn't thinking about that, although my parents called this morning asking us to bring Nicole and Timmy to their home for the holidays. That's what started me thinking about what's usually done here.''

"We have programs at both schools,'' Edna continued. "Curtis, I'd like for you to plan the one at The Crossroads.''

"Okay. I'll start working on it right away.''

"What do you do with the students who stay here?'' Summer asked. "There should be something special for them.''

"We buy a gift for each student, but sometimes it's not much. Depends on how much money we have left after the necessary bills are paid.''

"I'll ask my mother and sister in Ohio to send gifts for the students at The Crossroads. Autumn's church congregation will be glad to help I'm sure.''

"That will be fine,'' Edna said. "We rely heavily on contributions for our Christmas activities.''

"It disturbs me,'' Summer said, "that the schools operate from hand to mouth. There's surely some way we can provide a budget for the school so we'll know what we have to work with. I've been thinking about sending out a monthly newsletter to churches that support the schools. The older students could be involved with preparing it. Would the mission board supply a list of supporters and indicate how we can encourage additional support? I have a few acquaintances in New York who might even be interested in what we're doing.''

"It would be great if we could find a few large

contributors to make substantial bequests to an endowment fund and put The Crossroads on a self-supporting basis," David said.

"We operate on faith, David," Edna said quietly. "God supplies all our needs."

"I believe that, but I don't see that it's sacrilegious to provide these kids with more than the necessities. I envision the day when The Crossroads will have a big gym, so our students can compete in intramural sports, and additional dorm space to reach out to more youth. The volunteers are doing a good job, but it would be more effective if we had enough funds to pay a full-time staff. And that's never going to happen unless we publicize what we're doing. Summer's newsletter could do that. Do you actually believe it's wrong to work toward economic stability, Edna?"

She hesitated. "No. It's just not my concept of mission work, but I realize I've been here a long time. I may be out of touch with reality."

"You're doing a wonderful job, Edna," Summer said sincerely. "I can tell from Nicole and Timmy's progress that they couldn't receive a better elementary education anywhere, but I believe we have to make changes at The Crossroads."

Curtis nodded enthusiastically. "If there aren't some changes in the curriculum, Crossroads residents won't be prepared to face the challenges of the twenty-first century."

"Exactly," David said. "We need a computer lab, for one thing. And the science teacher is a wonderful person, but at seventy years, he's still teaching science and math as he did twenty years ago. That's not good enough anymore. We need staff members who have kept up with changes in technology."

Edna threw up her hands. "I apparently haven't kept up with the times, either. David, you and Summer are The Crossroads' administrators. You can make decisions, subject to the approval of the mission board. I'm in an advisory position only and overseer of the spiritual climate. I just want these schools to serve the purpose for which they were organized—a place for spiritual, physical and mental growth to youth who can't find it elsewhere. I'll be the first to concede that you may know how to do that better than I do. My methods are much like they were when I first came here."

"But they're working, so why change them?" Summer said.

Edna smiled her thanks at Summer. "I'll support your decisions as much as possible, but remember, all of you, that unless the motivation comes from God, your plans will never succeed."

Summer returned to her office after the conference ended, but it wasn't long before David wandered in, a bemused expression on his face. He perched on the edge of her desk.

"Do you realize what we were doing just now? We were making plans as if we intended to spend the rest of our lives at The Crossroads instead of the one year we promised."

Summer tapped a pencil on the edge of her desk. "Yes, and that disturbs me! After just a few weeks, I've become so wrapped up in the lives of these students and the work of the school that I hardly ever think of New York. It's like I've been transplanted to a new planet and my old life has been erased."

"I didn't know how much I was heading in that same direction until we had that meeting today. I'm constantly thinking about what needs to be done here.''

"I understand the dedication of Spring and Bert much better now. When you get caught up in other people's problems, you don't have time to think about yourself.''

"Both of us were self-centered, so perhaps this is a good lesson for us,'' he said.

"You mentioned that your parents want us to bring Nicole and Timmy for Christmas in Tennessee, but when there are students left here, I rather hate to leave them. How about inviting your parents to come and spend Christmas with us?''

David brightened. "How nice of you to think of that, Summer. It's been worrying me because my parents wouldn't have either of their sons for Christmas, but I hadn't thought of asking them to visit us. It really isn't a long drive from Nashville, and I think they'll come.'' He leaned over and brushed his lips over hers. "You're a sweetheart! Thanks.''

His touch was electrifying! Their gazes held and he put his hand on her shoulder and leaned over to kiss her again, but he drew back quickly when the office door opened and Edna walked in.

He felt so frustrated in his association with Summer. He'd looked forward to being at The Crossroads so they could explore a deeper relationship, but all of their time and conversation dealt with Timmy and Nicole or the administration of the school. They never had time for any personal communication.

Edna handed Summer a packet of mail she'd just gotten from the postman. And to cover the confusion she felt from David's kiss, Summer said, "I hope those are contributions rather than bills. Our funds are getting low.''

''God will provide,'' Edna said with confidence.

Edna closed the door behind her, and David tugged on Summer's arms until she stood in his tight embrace. The mystery in his eyes attracted her, but something cautioned her to resist him.

''No, David,'' she said fearfully, agitated by the strange surge of anticipation and the irregularity of her heartbeat. She struggled in his embrace, but his arms were like steel bands holding her close. David had always been so gentle before. She opened her mouth to protest, but he sealed her lips with his in a pleasurable kiss that Summer thought would never end. A caress that exhilarated her from the top of her head to the tips of her toes. Still holding her close, he lifted his lips and rested his chin on her soft hair.

When he realized that Summer was trembling in his embrace, he released her and lifted her chin. Her blue eyes brimmed with tears, reminding him of the ocean, and he was instantly contrite.

''Aw, Summer,'' he said, but she twisted away from him and ran out of the office. Angrily swiping the tears from her eyes, she hurried along the path to the cabin. Her heart was pounding rapidly, and she found it difficult to breathe. She stopped in her tracks when a disastrous thought entered her mind. Was she falling in love with David? She'd never felt this way about any other man. Summer covered her face with her hands and groaned. She had enough trouble without that.

She couldn't deal with this new emotion right now, and fearing that David might follow her, she dashed into the cabin and pulled a heavy jacket out of the closet. She put a granola bar and a bottle of water in her pocket and hurried away from the cabin and into the forest. She soon realized she'd gotten one of Spring's jackets instead of her own, but she walked on for a mile or two, her thoughts and senses numb to what had happened in the office. Summer had never intended to fall in love with anyone. If she did love David, that would certainly complicate her life.

She reached a stony outcropping and sat down in a place warmed by the sun. Nibbling on the granola, she thought of what had happened between her and David. She'd always liked his kisses before, but today's incident disturbed her so much because of her response to his kiss.

When Summer stuck the empty bar wrapper into her pocket, her hand encountered a book, and looking at it she saw it was a New Testament. Spring's name was on the cover. She clutched the volume as if it were a lifeline. She no longer had control of her life, and in her inadequacy, she needed God's guidance. What could she find to guide her in the present situation? She needed wisdom more than anything else, and in the past few weeks, Curtis's sermons had convinced her that direction for any situation could be found in the Bible.

She found the verse for her needs today in the first chapter of James. "If any of you lacks wisdom, he should ask God, who gives generously to all without finding fault, and it will be given to him. But when he asks, he must believe and not doubt, because he who doubts is like a wave of the sea, blown and tossed by the wind."

"God," Summer prayed aloud. "I need wisdom— wisdom to deal with Timmy and Nicole, but more than anything else, I need wisdom to know how to handle this new feeling I have for David. Amen.''

Spiritually, Summer still lacked a lot before she could be the kind of follower God could use, but she did believe He'd heard the yearnings of her heart. She left the glade with a calmer spirit than she'd had for weeks.

As she passed through the forest where the chapel was located, the young chaplain was approaching the building.

"Curtis," she said, "I'd like to talk with you sometime. I know you're here to work with the students, and I hate to add to your workload, but I have so many spiritual doubts, and no one to talk to about them except you and Edna."

"I'll be glad to help you. We'll find a time that's convenient for both of us." He patted her on the shoulder, making her feel like a child, rather than several years his senior.

David was already at the cabin, setting the table, when she returned.

"I have a casserole prepared," she said. "I'll put it in the oven." She looked at the clock. "The kids should be home."

"They asked me if they could play a while with their friends. I told them it would be all right."

Did he have any idea why she'd run away today? The easy camaraderie she and David had shared on previous evenings while they'd prepared the meal was gone. She wanted to speak, but she couldn't—their encounter earlier in the day stood in the way.

Fortunately, Timmy and Nicole soon came in, their

faces flushed from the cold wind. Timmy had his coat slung over his shoulder.

"Timmy! You should wear your coat," Summer said.

"I told him," Nicole said. "He's been playing without it since school was dismissed. He'll be sick."

"Timmy! Wear your coat from now on," David ordered.

"Okay!" he said grumpily and threw his coat on the floor.

Summer knew he'd done it deliberately to annoy her, but she didn't say anything as he turned on the television.

"Which reminds me, where's the nearest doctor if someone does get sick?"

She didn't direct the question to David, but he answered, "There's a resident nurse at the elementary school, who also helps out at The Crossroads when necessary, but the nearest hospital is in Asheville."

"Let's hope we don't need one, but thinking back to when we were children, it seems like one of us was sick most of the time during winter."

David watched television with Timmy, and took care of hearing the children's prayers. Wanting desperately to make amends for her attitude and to restore their easy fellowship, Summer walked with him to the door.

"I'm sorry I ran away this afternoon. I'm awfully confused. We're in an awkward situation."

David gave her a frank and admiring look and taking her hands he drew her toward him. "Forget everything about this afternoon except this," he said, and gathering her into his arms he held her snugly. His finger tenderly lifted her chin, and with eyes locking, his lips pressed against hers. "I know I was to go slow on the kisses, but I got carried away today. It'll be all right."

She hadn't yet gone to sleep when Timmy started coughing, but she lay still, hoping it would be temporary. In the middle of one severe coughing bout, he called, "Mommy."

Although the children called her Auntie all the time now, quite often at nighttime, Timmy would yell "Mommy," and she didn't know if he wanted her or was still thinking about Spring.

She shivered into a robe and went to the bedroom. Nicole was sleeping, but Timmy sat up in the bed, his blue eyes looking alarmed in the dim light.

"I'm sick, Auntie."

"I know." She put her hand on his forehead, and it was hot to her touch. Although she hadn't had any experience with doctoring children, she remembered what her mother had done when any of them had colds. She'd noticed that Spring had the same remedies in the medicine cabinet. "I'll see what I can find to make you better."

She gave him a spoonful of lemon-flavored cough syrup, a fever-reducing medicine, and rubbed his neck and chest with a medicated ointment—treatments that had always worked for the Weaver daughters.

"Lie down and try to sleep," Autumn said as she tucked the covers around him. "I'll sit on your bed until I'm sure you're asleep."

Timmy coughed several more times, but after an hour when he seemed to be breathing easier, Summer went back to her bed, but not to a deep sleep while she listened for Timmy to call. The next morning, he seemed better, but he still had a temperature, so she kept him home from school. She wrote David a note that she wouldn't be coming to work and sent it by Nicole when she started out.

She gave Timmy a bowl of hot chicken broth for breakfast, and then made a bed for him on the couch. He was watching cartoons when David came in.

He playfully cuffed Timmy on the top of the head. "Hey, are you being lazy this morning?"

"Nope. I'm sick. Ask Auntie."

"He's better now, but he coughed a lot in the night, and he still has some temperature. Sorry to leave you with all the office work, but I thought he should stay home."

"You don't look like you had much rest, either," he said as he poured a cup of coffee and sat down on the sofa beside Timmy.

"No, not much," she agreed. "The cough syrup will make Timmy drowsy, and when he goes to sleep, I'll take a nap."

"No way!" Timmy said. "I'm gonna watch television all morning." Summer didn't respond for she'd learned that even if Timmy did put up a protest, however reluctantly, he always did what she told him.

Chapter Twelve

Edna had gotten a list of sponsors from the mission board, along with the permission to circulate a newsletter. David and Summer added names of their extended families, and impulsively she added the name of Mr. Abel in New York. Anita, Mayo and Skipper volunteered to help with the newsletter, and they were so thrilled with the project that they were willing to forgo their television programs, and every night for a week, Summer left David to oversee the children while she went to the office to work on the newsletter.

Skipper turned out to be proficient on the computer, and he was so excited to be working with Summer's equipment that he begged to be allowed to design the masthead.

They'd agreed to head the newsletter, *The Crossroads,* with Galatians 6:10 quoted under the title, ''As often as we have the chance we should do good to everyone, but especially to those who belong to our family in the faith.''

Skipper sketched in the rustic chapel on one side

of the title, and on the other side, he illustrated the meeting of two roads. He had a lot of talent, and Summer was thankful that he'd come to The Crossroads where he would find the right direction for his life. The longer she worked at the school, the more she was convinced of the necessity for this type of institution. And according to the director of the mission board, they had applications every day for youth who needed a place to go, but The Crossroads couldn't accommodate anymore residents. Even if the school didn't reach the potential David and Summer envisioned, if more people knew about their work, perhaps monetary contributions would increase.

Anita circulated among the classes and wrote several articles about the work of the school. Summer made a few suggestions and corrections on grammar and punctuation, but basically, it was Anita's composition.

Using a camera his father had given him, Mayo Sinclair discussed taking a picture of one of The Crossroads' volunteers and scanning it into the paper.

"Why don't you do an article on Hallie Blackburn?" Summer suggested. "She does a lot of hard work for very little pay, and I doubt she ever has compliments from any of you students. It would please her."

"She won't let me take her picture," Mayo said.

"Then why not take a picture of the kitchen and put that in the paper. It wouldn't hurt our readers to see that Hallie could use some new equipment."

"Say! That's not a bad idea. I'll talk to her right away."

They mailed the first issue the week after Thanksgiving, hoping to influence churches to increase their allocation to the school when they made their yearly budgets. While not counting too much on immediate results, Summer and David believed the newsletter would eventually benefit the school.

When David came in for supper on the first day of December, he said, "Have you heard the weather forecast?"

Summer was dropping biscuits on top of a chicken pot pie, and she said, "No, the children are still at school, and I haven't turned on the television."

"We're supposed to have a foot or more of snow tonight and tomorrow."

"That will really isolate us, won't it?" Summer said in concern. She couldn't get over her fear of being cut off from the rest of the world.

"Maybe, for a few days."

"I'll go back to the office and telephone my parents tonight. They'll worry about us if we do have a bad storm."

"That's a good idea for the telephone lines could go down in a deep snow. Ask your folks to telephone Mom and Dad, so they'll know we're all right."

Summer heard the wind rising during the night, and in spite of the heat from the gas furnace in the hallway, the house was cold. She was thankful that, a few weeks ago, David had hired Stonewall to provide logs for the fireplace, and Stonewall had stacked the wood on the porch, so they'd have easy access to it. If they lost electric power, the thermostat on the furnace wouldn't work, but they could have some heat from the fireplace. Blowing snow splattered against the windows, and she expected a white world by morning.

She was still in bed when she heard steps on the porch and David called, "Summer."

She put on her robe and opened the door for him. He was bundled in a heavy parka, covered with snow, and his eyes glowed with enjoyment.

"Everything okay?" he said. He shook the snow off his coat before he came into the cabin.

"It got cold in here during the night, and I thought I might have to light the wood in the fireplace. Is there a lot of snow?"

"About six inches and still coming down. This is the kind of snow that pulls trees down on the electricity lines, but I didn't see any broken limbs along the trail."

Summer flipped a switch, and the ceiling light came on. "At least we have a gas stove, so we can cook if the power goes off. Will we have school as usual?"

"As far as I know. One of the volunteers is cleaning off the grounds with a tractor and snowplow. We might have to use snowshoes to travel around the compound if the snow gets much deeper."

She eyed him, amazed at his enthusiasm. "The more I'm around you, the more I'm aware of how different our outlooks on life are."

"Have you been looking for differences?"

"Not particularly, but I can't help notice. Now, for instance. You're as excited about this snow as if you were a kid looking for Santa Claus. I tend to be more practical, wondering if we'll have enough food to last until the snow melts, trying to figure out how to cope if we lose electric power, concerned about how to get to a doctor if one of the kids get sick."

"Why worry about things that may never happen?"

"A little foresight can be handy."

"I had extra wood laid in a few weeks ago," David defended himself.

"I guess you did at that," she admitted with a smile. "If we have any problems, I'll expect you to deal with them. So go ahead and enjoy the snow. I suppose you'll be building a snowman."

"As soon as school's out today, I'll take Timmy and Nicole out on the point and build a huge—" he measured with his hands "—snowman to overlook the valley. And furthermore," he tweaked her chin, "I expect you to help us."

"Then I'd better get dressed and wake the family."

When she returned to the kitchen, David had laid his heavy coat aside. A pot of coffee was perking, four places were arranged at the table, juice was poured and he was making toast.

"Thought I'd invite myself for breakfast. With this storm, Hallie may not make it off the mountain and breakfast will be sparse at The Crossroads."

"You know, you're a right handy man to have around the house," she said with an approving smile. "I don't suppose my father has ever made a pot of coffee in his life, and I'm sure he's never even poured out a bowl of cereal for himself."

"But you've always had a housekeeper. My parents both worked outside the home, and after we kids were in our teens, it was everyone for himself for breakfast and lunch. Mom prepared a balanced evening meal when all of us sat down and ate together."

By noon, the snow had almost stopped, but it was

still cloudy and the wind intensified throughout the afternoon. Edna stopped by the office.

"I'd better tell you about our procedure in case the electricity goes off, which it probably will when this heavy snow starts falling off the trees onto the power lines. Gas generators provide alternate power for the two schools, but we only use them to provide heat to the dormitories. Which means, if the electricity goes off, we won't be having school."

"Then what?" David asked.

"We declare a school holiday. We keep a lot of puzzles and table games, and try to entertain the smaller children inside, or let them make snowmen and have snowball fights. The older students play outdoors—skiing around the meadow, snowshoeing in the valley, sleigh riding. Occasionally the lake freezes solid, and they go ice-skating. A few times we've been without power for a week or more, but usually it's no more than a couple of days."

The electricity went off in midafternoon, and the administration building shook slightly from the concerted rejoicing of the thirty students who shouted in unison. When an hour passed and the power hadn't been restored, Summer said, "I might as well go to the cabin for we can't do anything here without electricity."

"That's fine," David agreed, "I'll collect the kids and bring them home. Probably the path is filled with snow again." He hesitated. "I don't like for you to be stuck with all the responsibility of keeping a fire going. Under the circumstances, I don't see any reason why I can't stay at the cabin until the weather clears up."

Her mouth quirked with humor. "I can't believe Edna will object."

An undefinable emotion gleamed in his brown eyes. "I wasn't thinking about Edna. Is it all right with *you?*"

"Yes," she said briefly, but she felt her composure was under attack. Since she'd started thinking she might be in love with David, she didn't know how she would manage with being cooped up in the cabin with him for several days.

"If we don't have electric power, we won't have any water at the cabin, so I'll ask one of the men to bring a tank of water on the tractor. Unless you want to do like the pioneers and melt snow over the fire."

Summer's gentle laugh rippled through the dark office. "To think that I used to resent living with my family, and I longed to get out on my own. I can't believe I'm now responsible for making decisions for more than thirty people!"

"Summer, do you realize how much you've changed since we came here two months ago? You've adjusted to a situation that's completely opposed to your nature." Putting his arms around her waist, he squeezed her affectionately. "You often compare yourself unworthily to your sisters, but you shouldn't. You're a pretty special person, and I don't think either one of them would have handled this situation any better than you have."

"Thanks. I've made lots of mistakes, but I've tried to do my best. I couldn't have done it without your help."

David never caressed her unless they were alone, and knowing they wouldn't have any privacy the next few days, she cuddled against him and lifted her face for a kiss—for the first time taking the initiative in their increasing infatuation. Ecstacy raced through her body from the sweet tenderness of his kiss, and he sighed contentedly when he released her.

"I'll feel much more secure with you in the cabin," she said softly.

For the past few years, Summer had anticipated the time when she wouldn't have to depend on anyone. In the past she'd been forced to rely on her parents, but since the deaths of Bert and Spring, she'd developed her own strength of character. She'd made a lot of difficult decisions, and she was convinced that she did have the fortitude to cope with snowstorms, rebellious teenagers and mischievous children. She *could* do it alone, but it was much more satisfactory to have David beside her.

As a child, Summer had spent a lot of time puttering around in the kitchen trying to help their longtime housekeeper, so she had some knowledge of cooking skills, but she lacked practice. Since she was home early, she got out the cookbook she'd bought before she left New York, looking for some kind of special treat for the evening meal. The cabin was dark, but there was a kerosene lamp on the mantel, and she brought it to the kitchen area.

She decided on a menu of baked steak, mashed potatoes, buttered corn and apple salad for dinner, and tried her hand at making rolls. While the food cooked, she put a tablecloth on the table, took some candles and holders from one of the cabinets and arranged them with the silverware. Surveying her efforts, she said aloud, "It doesn't look like a Weaver table, but it'll have to do."

Without television, she had to think of a way to entertain Nicole and Timmy for the evening. She remembered seeing a few table games somewhere in the cabin, and she found them behind boxes stored in the hall closet. These would probably keep the kids occupied until bedtime.

Nicole and Timmy were quarreling as they came down the path because Timmy had rubbed a handful of snow in Nicole's face.

"I'm going to get even with you," Nicole shouted as Timmy ran up on the porch, taunting her. She wadded a big batch of snow in both hands and threw it just as he opened the door and dodged inside. The snow came through the open doorway and splattered on the floor.

"Stop it!" Summer called. Timmy was tramping around the room dripping snow as he went. "Timmy, take off your boots and help clean up that snow."

"She pitched it—not me," he said.

"Matters not. You made your sister mad, or she wouldn't have thrown snow at you. Hurry! I want both of you to get out of your damp clothes and wipe the floor."

Order was restored by the time David came, and it was almost dark then. He carried a duffel roll over his shoulder, which he dropped beside the fireplace.

"Hey! Look, kids, we're going to dine at the Ritz tonight—candles 'n' everything," he said as Summer lit the candles.

Timmy came running. "Supper smells good," he said, climbing into his chair.

When Nicole came, her cheeks still glowing from the snow, David held the chair for Summer before he sat down. Without any other light, it seemed as if the four of them were wrapped in a world of their own. Looking around at her companions, Summer was breathless to realize that there was no other place she'd rather be right now. She reached her hands to Timmy and David, and noting her intent, he joined hands with Nicole, who then clasped Timmy's hand.

"Why don't you say the blessing tonight, David? We do have so much to be thankful for."

He nodded solemnly and squeezed her hand until it hurt.

"God, thank You for bringing us together as a—" he paused "—family. We're thankful for this snowstorm and the opportunity to shut out the rest of the world and focus on each other. We're thankful for the food, and for Summer who's prepared it. Amen."

There was still enough hot water in the tank to wash the dishes, and Summer assigned everyone a part in cleaning up the kitchen table and cabinets. Cold was seeping into the cabin, and she thought the children should keep busy.

After the evening meal, Summer spread blankets near the open fire and filled the wire popper hanging on the fireplace with grains of corn. Although she limited the soda consumption of the children, earlier she'd set a two-liter bottle of cola on the porch. When the corn was ready, she brought in the cola.

"We did this last winter with Mommy and Daddy," Nicole said. She moved close to Summer and gave her a hug. "Thanks, Auntie."

Summer smothered a sob. It was the first time either of the children had shown any appreciation of what she was doing for them. David's gaze was gentle and understanding, and she knew he was conscious of the satisfaction she'd experienced at Nicole's words.

"I thought we might work on these jigsaw puzzles," she said, bringing out two boxes. The pieces were quite large, and she thought even Timmy would enjoy them.

"Let's have two teams and see who can finish their puzzles first," Summer suggested. "How about girls against the boys?"

"We'll beat them, won't we, Uncle David?" Timmy said.

"Oh, I don't know. Girls are pretty tricky, and I'm a little rusty on jigsaw puzzle skills."

David and Timmy moved to one side of the blanket and Summer poured out the puzzle pieces in two piles. "Turn the pieces right side up, but no starting until I give the signal."

Summer and Nicole finished first, which caused an argument between Nicole and Timmy.

"They had the easiest puzzle," Timmy said, pouting.

"Then we'll switch puzzles and try again," Summer said. But when the ladies' team finished first again, David said to Timmy, "They just outclass us, partner. We're still best about a lot of things."

"Let's play bingo," Summer said. "We can take turns calling the numbers."

"Timmy doesn't know all his numbers," Nicole objected.

"Then one of us will help him when it's his turn," David said. "What are we going to have for prizes? I feel lucky this time."

"I have a bag of chocolate kisses, but they're not

to be eaten this late at night. We don't need any hyper kids, or adults, in the cabin this close to bedtime.''

"You mean I can't have a kiss if I win?" David said, mimicking Timmy's pouting voice, but his eyes brimmed with mirth.

Summer knew he wasn't talking about the candy kisses, and she answered pertly, "No kisses tonight."

The hours passed quickly, and Summer was only occasionally aware of the strong wind whipping around the cabin. They stopped playing often while David added logs to the fire.

When Summer mentioned bedtime, perhaps hoping to postpone the inevitable, Timmy said, "Sometimes Daddy used to tell us Bible stories before we went to bed."

David and Summer exchanged glances, and she shrugged her shoulders. "I guess I can come up with a Bible story I learned in Sunday school," David said.

Timmy scooted across the floor until he leaned against David.

"There was this little Hebrew baby named Moses," David began, "and a mean old king was trying to kill him. But his mother made up her mind that her boy was going to be taken care of, so she built a little boat and put the baby in it. She hid the boat in the river, and when the king's daughter came down to the water, she saw the baby. The princess knew her father wanted to kill all the little Hebrew babies, but she didn't have a child of her own, so she sneaked Moses into the palace and pretended he was hers. But she didn't know how to take care of a baby, so the king's daughter looked for somebody else to watch over Moses until he was older. God made it possible for the princess to choose Moses's real mother to take care of him. He grew up to be a good man, and God had great work for Moses to do. So Moses was better off than lots of babies. He had two mothers to love him.''

When David finished the story, Timmy's face split into a wide grin. "Just like me and Nicole. We had Mommy, and now we have Auntie. God's looking out for us, too.''

He rushed over to Summer, put his arms around her and kissed her. Summer held him tightly, her eyes closed to hold back the threatening tears. Overwhelmed by the warm glow that flowed through her, she softly paddled Timmy's rump.

"But I'll not be a very good mother if I don't see that you get into bed for a good night's sleep. Come on, I'll help you get ready for bed. It's going to be dark in the cabin tonight, but Uncle David and I'll both be here to watch over you.''

"God will be, too," Nicole said.

"And that's the most important," Summer agreed.

Chapter Thirteen

When she returned to the living room after settling the children, David was carrying wood in from the porch and stacking it near the fireplace. He spread his sleeping bag out on the floor.

"You can sleep on the sofa, if you like," Summer said.

"No, I'll roll up in front of the fire. I have a feeling the temperature will drop rapidly tonight, and if I'm lying here, I'll know when I need to add fuel. Leave the hall door and the bedroom doors open so the heat can circulate. I checked the thermometer on the porch, and it's registering at zero."

"Brrr!" Summer said and shivered. "I hope we can stay warm. I piled a lot of blankets on the kids' beds until Nicole complained she couldn't move. I've laid another blanket on the sofa if you need it. I'm going to bed, too."

Summer had extinguished the candles, except for the one she held in her hand. David stood in the shadows, but a flicker of firelight caught the tenderness and passion in his eyes. He held out his hand.

"No need to be in a hurry. It's a long time until morning."

Her pulses surged with excitement, and she said slowly, "No, David, I don't think so." But even as she spoke, she put the candle on the table and moved toward him, drawn by an instinctive response that she couldn't have suppressed if she'd wanted to.

With one swift motion, she was in his arms, and he whispered into her hair, "It's all right, Summer. It's all right."

And being in David's arms did make everything all right. He turned the large lounge chair to face the fire, and he drew her down beside him.

"You're not much bigger than Timmy," he said with a chuckle, "so both of us can sit in this chair." He draped a blanket around them and their mutual warmth kept the cold at bay as they cuddled up in each other's arms.

"This is the first time I've snuggled like this with a woman in my arms. I kinda like it."

Summer nodded her head, and her soft, silky hair tickled his chin. "'Specially on a cold night."

"How about you?"

She lifted her head and stared at him. "You mean, have I cuddled in another man's arms? Of course not. I haven't dated anyone since I left high school."

"Have you ever wondered why we're so comfortable together?"

"I don't want to think about it. I'd just as soon think we're comfortable this way because it's such a cold night. I'm not ready to explore any other possibility."

"Why?"

"It disturbs me to realize how much my life has changed in the past few months. It's only been four months since Spring and Bert died, and sometimes I have to force myself to remember that I've ever had any life except this one."

"You told me when we came to The Crossroads for the first time that you were terrified, as if the mountains were closing around you and you'd never get out."

"That's the way it is, too, but it's not as terrible as I thought it might be. Spring had her Christian calling to keep her at The Crossroads, but that's not why I'm staying."

"Do you want to explore your reasons?"

"Not tonight. That's something I have to face in broad daylight—not in a fairy-tale setting like this one."

David decided not to press her further. He suppressed his emotions and desires, being content that she trusted him enough to go to sleep in his arms. When the fire had burned to embers, David released Summer to lay more logs on the coals.

She straightened, yawning, looking vulnerable and desirable in the faint light. "What time is it?" she asked.

"One o'clock."

"I didn't know I'd gone to sleep. Good night, David."

Keeping his distance, he said, "Good night. Call if you need me."

Her bedroom was frigid, and as Summer tried to go to sleep again, she was aware of the swirling wind outside the window; but more than that, she felt comforted because David was nearby. He'd become such an important part of her life that she wondered where the future was leading them. If they stayed on at The Crossroads more than a year, could their relationship continue as it was now? If at the end of a year, they decided they could no longer manage The Crossroads, and they each went their separate ways again, how much would she care?

Also distressed by her reaction to Timmy's affection, Summer knew how important the children had become to her. Her sleep was troubled, and she was aware several times when David laid logs on the fire, and even then the cabin seemed cold. Daylight crept into the cabin, and Summer put on a heavy robe and walked into the kitchen quietly, not wanting to disturb anyone else.

Also awake, David said softly, "Nice and clear outside." He enjoyed the sight of Summer's tousled hair and her sleep-swollen eyes. She seldom had a hair out of place, and even to a man as fastidious in his dress as he was, he thought she would seem more human if she wasn't always as neat as a pin. More than once, his hands had itched to run his fingers through her carefully groomed hair.

Summer moved close to the fireplace and glanced toward the kitchen window that was plastered with snow.

David threw back the top of the sleeping bag, and she saw he'd slept in his clothes. "I'll bring in some more wood now that you're awake," he offered, and while he carried out the ashes and brought in more wood, she went to the bathroom to dress. The wooden floor was cold on her bare feet, and she put on her heaviest sweat outfit and fleece-lined boots. The bedroom area was frigid, but she peeked in and saw that Nicole and Timmy were still asleep, so she knew they were comfortable.

"Wow!" David said when he came in with an armload of logs. "It's a degree above zero, so it'll be a cold day."

"Since we aren't in a hurry, how about eggs and biscuits for breakfast? I bought a bag of biscuit mix a few weeks ago."

"Sounds good to me."

Before they'd finished breakfast, they heard loud voices approaching the cabin, and soon heavy steps on the porch. David grinned. "The natives are already astir."

Skipper opened the door, a huge smile spread across his face. He had on a red jacket with a cap pulled over his ears. "C'mon, guys. We're going sleigh riding."

"We can't go until we've had breakfast," Summer said. "Come in and close the door."

Skipper stomped the snow off his feet and came inside, followed by Mayo, Anita and several other students.

Anita sniffed appreciatively. "Those biscuits look good. Hallie didn't make it off the mountain, so we had nothing but a slice of bread and jelly for breakfast."

"I can take a hint," Summer said. "I'll make another batch."

The boys yelled, "Way to go," and they pulled off their heavy coats and piled them by the door.

"Sorry there aren't enough chairs for everybody," David said, as he took plates and cups from the cabinets.

"No problem!" Mayo said. "We'll eat standing up."

David scrambled a dozen eggs, and Summer was glad she'd laid in an extra supply of food the last time they'd gone into Asheville. Hopefully, they wouldn't run out before the snow melted enough for them to get off the mountain. But she tried not to think about her limited supply of food or money when she saw how much the young people enjoyed the biscuits and eggs.

"Say, David," Anita said, "can we take some food from the kitchen, have a bonfire and eat outdoors tonight? It would cost the same whether we ate inside or out."

"I don't know why not," he said, "but I'm new at this. I'll run it by Edna."

"Where would we have the fire?" Summer asked.

"Down by the lake is the best place. Maybe Curtis could have a vesper service."

"It's going to be mighty cold, but I'll go along if Edna approves it," David said.

After getting a promise from David and Summer that they'd join them after they'd made the snowman David had promised the kids, the teenagers headed on toward the valley area. Their merrymaking had awakened Timmy and Nicole, and David and Summer made more biscuits and eggs for the kids because their unexpected guests had eaten everything in sight. Then they had to heat water and wash all the dishes.

"Whew!" Summer said when they finished and she collapsed on the couch. "I'm glad I don't have to cook for that bunch every day."

"But they did enjoy it," David said.

"Surprising as it might seem, so did I. It's the

home atmosphere as much as the food. How much would it stretch our budget to entertain all the students once a month? You're handy in the kitchen, and the two of us together should be able to come up with enough food to satisfy their big appetites. We could have soups, spaghetti or lasagna—that type of food, with salad and desserts.''

David sat beside her and kissed her on the forehead. ''You're sweet to even think of it! They love to come to the cabin. Do you think we can wedge thirty people in, besides the four who are already eating here?''

''We could try it one time, and if it's too crowded, we can have half of them one week and half the next. I don't want to do it more often than that for it wouldn't be fair to Timmy and Nicole.''

His eyes were tender as he looked at her. ''Summer, do you ever think about yourself?''

''Not anymore, it seems. I don't have time.''

He reached out and ruffled her hair, what he'd been wanting to do for a long time, and she didn't protest. ''Get your heavy clothes on. Let's go play in the snow. I intend to rub snow in your face.''

She made a face at him. ''You won't have to. I'm sure Mayo and Skipper will beat you to it. But at least you've warned me, so I'll put a lot of lotion and cream on my face.''

The power was off for three days and The Crossroads students spent every daylight hour outdoors. Since there wasn't anything else Summer could do, she went with them. She tried walking on snowshoes, which she found exhilarating. She attempted skiing and gave it up as a poor job. She slid down a small slope on rickety handmade sleds, the hood of an auto and a commercially made sled that was in shambles at the end of two days. None of those things she'd tried before, and she was surprised at how much she enjoyed herself.

Summer often noticed David watching her with a glint of wonder in his eyes. Once when he helped her up after she'd tumbled off a sled, he whispered, "I knew I'd find the woman I remembered if I waited long enough," referring to the first time they'd met.

Once the power was restored and school was in session, everyone's thoughts turned to Christmas. Curtis planned a program for the night before school was dismissed, because about half the student body would be going to spend the holiday with relatives.

Summer made an effort to enter into the Christmas plans, but as the holiday came closer, her spirits plummeted. This would be the first time she hadn't spent Christmas at home, and she kept thinking about the years gone by when she hadn't appreciated her home as much as she should have.

Guessing her problem, David said, "There's no reason you can't go home for a few days, Summer. My folks are coming, and they can help me look after Nicole and Timmy."

"No, I won't do that, but I appreciate your offer."

Although she and David realized that the Christmas season would be easier for both their families if they were with them, they'd decided their responsibilities lay with the students who would also miss Spring and Bert.

Just having David understand that she was homesick soothed her, and when several cartons of gifts arrived from Summer's family, she threw off her dismal mood and entered into the local plans with enthusiasm. Checking to see that every student had a gift suited especially for them, she and David made plans for a Christmas party.

"We need a tree for the cafeteria," Summer said. "And a small one for the cabin."

"There's a grove of evergreens on the compound's property at the upper end of the valley. I'm sure we can find what we need there. The boys can get one for the cafeteria, but let's make it a family outing to get a tree for the cabin. Going after the Christmas tree used to be a highlight for our family."

"Sounds good to me. Let's wait until the Saturday before Christmas. A tree is going to crowd the cabin even more than it is now, and once we get the tree decorated, I know the kids won't want to take it down very soon."

"Do we have any decorations?"

"There's a box of lights and ornaments in the cabin, and I'll find out from Edna if any are available for the cafeteria. If not, we'll make some. I should be creative enough to come up with an idea for decorations from all the plastic bottles we have around here."

"The students usually have good ideas, too."

"David, let's plan something special for those who have to stay here during the holidays. Mother and Daddy sent me a check for five hundred dollars, so let's use that to take the students to see the Vanderbilt mansion in Asheville."

"It would be a treat for them to see Biltmore, but isn't that money your Christmas gift?"

Leaning back in her chair and lightly drumming her fingers on the desk, she said, "Yes. So that means I can do what I want to with it. Mother suggested that I buy clothes, but I won't spend that money on myself when these kids don't have anything new. I considered using it to buy clothes for the female students, but it wouldn't go very far. Besides, I'd rather include everyone if possible.''

"I don't see why we couldn't. We can probably get a school rate to tour the estate. We could take our van and the bus from the elementary school.''

"There would be twenty, counting the two of us, Nicole and Timmy. If we go while your parents are here, that would be two more.''

"Summer, when we came here you had so little understanding of what it meant to be a Christian, but I've seen a tremendous change in you. Have you had a change of heart?''

"I've been talking with Curtis about my spiritual needs, and he's been helpful. I'm reading Spring's Bible, especially the passages she's underlined, but I don't seem to be learning very fast. I've had such a long way to go.''

"I wonder if we aren't trying to do all of this by ourselves rather than depending on God for help. When we accept Christ as our Savior, the Holy Spirit comes to live in us, and He guides us in our decisions. It makes our way so much easier when we turn our whole lives over to God.''

"You're probably right,'' Summer agreed. "But when you grow up with a mother like mine who taught her daughters to be self-sufficient, it's hard to put your trust elsewhere. I know now that Mother wasn't always right, but it's hard to break a lifetime habit.''

"You've been terrific in taking over your duties

here. I know Bert and Spring would be pleased with
what we're doing. I came here because I thought I
owed it to them, but as the days go by, I'm learning
what I'm doing isn't so much for Bert and Spring, as
for Jesus. He said once that 'Whatever you did for
one of the least of these brothers of mine, you did for
me.' We might be putting the cart before the horse in
serving God before we've totally submitted our lives
to Him, but we're heading in the right direction.''

The excitement among the elementary school children and the teenagers at The Crossroads grew with
each day, and Summer was inspired by their enthusiasm. Christmas had always been an important day
at the Weaver home. Clara had decorated the house
lavishly, and the food was abundant, but it had all
been for their close-knit family. Occasionally, Clara
would invite her sister and family for Christmas dinner, but usually there were only the five Weavers.
And there was never any emphasis on the *real* meaning of Christmas. No Bible stories were read, although Summer had heard the other traditional Christmas stories.

At The Crossroads, all the holiday preparations revolved around the Biblical concept of Christmas.
Scriptures about Christ's birth were read over the in-
tercom every morning with a traditional carol following. Summer couldn't have avoided the emphasis on
Christ's birth if she'd wanted to, and she found she
didn't want to anymore.

The night before school was dismissed for a couple
of weeks, the celebration started with a traditional
dinner of turkey, dressing, hot rolls, vegetables, salad
and cherry pie. Although Hallie was generally a dour

person, even she loosened up and actually seemed to enjoy preparing the big meal.

One whole side of the cafeteria had been set aside for the Christmas tree. Summer had squeezed enough from The Crossroads budget to buy a gift for each student, the staff and volunteers, and with the gifts her mother and sister had sent, packages dominated one corner of the cafeteria. A well-wisher had sent several crates of apples and forty pounds of candy, so those items were distributed equally. Some of the teenagers had received packages from home, but they had been dispensed individually in the dorms at the discretion of the house parents. Mayo's father had sent him a banjo, which he brought to the party and accompanied the group in a series of Christmas carols.

"Mayo is sad," Anita whispered in Summer's ear. "His father had promised to take him for the holidays, but he isn't coming. He likes the banjo, but he'd rather have his dad."

No one wanted the party to end, but an inspirational service was planned at the chapel, so the party had to stop by ten o'clock.

As they went to the chapel, Summer held Nicole's hand, and David walked behind them, timing his steps to Timmy's. They'd gradually become like a family, and Summer often wondered if Timmy and Nicole even remembered their parents. Timmy sometimes called David, Daddy, and he hadn't corrected him. She supposed that in appearance and temperament she and David were enough like their parents that the children couldn't see much difference. David often came for breakfast, and he was there every evening, so the children saw as much of him as they had of

Bert. It was a strange arrangement, Summer thought, and she wished she knew where it was leading.

As the service opened, Mayo used his new banjo to accompany Anita as she sang a Christmas hymn. David looked at Summer in the dim light and lifted his eyebrows. She'd had no idea that Anita had such a beautiful voice. Anita was a part of the school chorus, and the group sang at chapel each week, but this was the first time she'd heard Anita sing a solo.

Wouldn't it be wonderful if Anita could pursue a career in music! If she took her to New York, she could arrange for her education. It had been a long time since Summer had contemplated returning to New York.

Summer listened to the lyrics of the hymns being sung by the group, and certain words leaped out at her until she could almost see the advent of Christ unfold as if she had been in Bethlehem on the night of his birth.

Curtis's short sermon was based on the Scripture, "Behold, I stand at the door and knock." Summer listened intently to the message, particularly when he closed with the words, "Jesus came into the world many years ago, but unless you've opened your heart to receive Him, Jesus hasn't come for you. The shepherds and the Wise Men knelt and worshiped Jesus. Let me repeat, if Jesus doesn't rule in your heart, He hasn't come for you, and you haven't experienced the full meaning of Christmas. Come and kneel at His feet tonight.

"As Mayo plays a closing hymn, if you really want to know the peace that Christ offers, come forward and acknowledge that you've accepted the gift God has for you. 'The gift of God is eternal life in Christ Jesus our Lord.'"

Staring straight ahead, with her heart pounding furiously, Summer saw several students go forward. Impulsively, she stepped past the children and David and walked automatically along the short aisle. Curtis was talking with one of the students, so Summer knelt at the small altar, eyes closed, head bowed in her hands. She sensed a presence at her side, and when a gentle hand was placed on her shoulder, even without looking, she knew that David knelt beside her.

When Mayo stopped the music, Summer and David stood with three students who'd come forward.

Curtis put his arms around their shoulders, and asked quietly, "Would you prefer that I talk with you privately about your experience, rather than before the students? I don't believe they're aware of the spiritual doubts you've had."

Summer nodded, and David said, "That would be best. Do you have time to come to the cabin tonight?"

"Of course."

"Whenever it's convenient," David said. "Go ahead and talk to the students first. It will take us a while to get Timmy and Nicole to bed."

Summer had hot chocolate made when Curtis breezed into the cabin, his smooth features more animated than usual.

"There must be rejoicing in Heaven—three more souls added to the kingdom tonight. Or perhaps five! Depending on what you have to tell me."

When they gathered around the kitchen table, cups of hot chocolate in their hands, David said, "As for me, I was born into the kingdom when I was a boy, but I haven't been living a Christian life as I should have. Tonight, I made a full commitment to live the rest of my life following the path Jesus laid out for me. I've known for a long time how I should live—I just haven't done it.''

"Some Christians approach all decisions by asking, 'What would Jesus do?'''

"Yes, and that's the way I intend to live from now on.''

"Summer?'' Curtis turned toward her.

Her voice broke slightly when she answered. ''I can't explain what happened exactly, but when you were speaking, I had the overwhelming certainty that Jesus *had* come into the world for *me*. The spiritual doubts I've had were suddenly gone, and I felt at peace. I don't understand much more than that, but many of the Scriptures I've been reading in the Bible the past few months took on new meaning.''

"Such as?'' Curtis prompted.

"'If the Son sets you free, you will be free indeed,' and 'Where the Spirit of the Lord is, there is freedom.''' A bemused expression crossed her face. "And it's odd that I should feel *free* because in accepting Jesus as my Savior, I'm really making Him Lord of my life, so I'll never be free to do what *I* want to again.'' Casting questioning eyes at Curtis, she said, ''At least that's the way I interpret it.''

Curtis laughed joyously. "You've summarized the meaning of the new life in Jesus Christ in a few words, Summer. From now on, you're under the Lordship of Christ.''

The three of them knelt, holding hands, and Curtis prayed for them.

"Lord," Curtis prayed, "this is the beginning of a new life for David and Summer, and although it takes only a short time to become a Christian, it takes a lifetime to become the kind of follower You'd have us to be. Help them to understand that doubts and problems will still come, but from now on, You'll be in control, and they can follow Your leading. Thank You for their commitment to The Crossroads and the difference they're making in the lives of the students they minister to. Amen."

When he put on his coat to leave, Curtis said, "You'll never forget this Christmas! When the way gets rough and the answers hard to find, remember what you've experienced tonight."

"If you're all right, Summer," David said, "I'll walk back to the dorm with Curtis. You may want to be alone now."

She smiled at his understanding, and the cabin seemed unusually quiet after they left, but Summer didn't mind the stillness. It gave her time to mull over the miracle of Christmas that had changed her life tonight.

Chapter Fourteen

Summer had a week to get ready for Christmas Day after school was dismissed. The house parents were staying with those students left in the dorms, but Anita spent a lot of the time at the cabin and Summer was glad to have her help. She took care of cleaning the house while Summer baked, and it was pleasant to have Anita for company. In spite of the difference in their ages, they'd become good friends.

"The Blackburns asked me to spend Christmas with them," Anita said one day.

"I overheard Hallie telling your housemother that she intended to ask you."

"Do you think I should go?"

"I don't have an opinion. I know very little about the Blackburns. Have you asked Edna? She's been here a long time, and she'd know whether it's a suitable place for you. Hallie can be cantankerous, but basically, I believe she's a good person."

"She likes me and she's hinted that they'd give me a home when I have to leave The Crossroads after I graduate. They don't have any kids, and I think Hallie's worrying because they won't have anybody to take care of them in their old age. But I don't want to spend the rest of my life in these mountains—there's a big world out there waiting for me.''

The comment amused Summer. How much that sounded like her own attitude when she was eighteen!

''I don't want to live with the Blackburns,'' Anita continued, ''but I do think I'll spend Christmas Day at their house. It will be a break from the usual routine.''

Anita might be angling for an invitation to spend Christmas at the cabin, but Summer didn't ask her because she thought it was best for Timmy and Nicole to have some uninterrupted time with their grandparents.

As David and Summer made their plans, she hoped there wouldn't be a repeat of the big snowstorm they'd had the first week of the month. After that heavy blast of winter, the weather moderated, and although the higher mountains didn't lose their snow and the valley still had lots of snowdrifts, the county roads were cleared. The area was beautiful, and Summer realized that she no longer looked upon the mountains as a prison.

Three days before Christmas, when a few snow flurries buffeted by a strong wind danced in the air, the Browns and Summer set out to find a Christmas tree for the cabin. Summer had expected they'd walk and carry the tree, but when David arrived, he was driving the compound's tractor with a low wagon attached.

Timmy and Nicole bolted out of the cabin.

"Just like Grandpa's farm," Timmy shouted.

"David, do you know how to drive a tractor?" Summer asked suspiciously.

"I'm driving this one," he said.

"Have you ever driven a tractor before?" she yelled above the noise of the engine.

"Well, no," he said, a mischievous gleam in his brown eyes, "but it can't be much different than driving a car. If you don't trust my skill, you can drive. You grew up on a farm."

"No, thanks. Autumn was the farm worker. Besides, when I was growing up, Daddy used his Belgian horses more than tractors."

Nicole had already climbed on the low wagon and pulled Timmy beside her. "Come on, Auntie," she called. "It'll be fun."

With a skeptical glance at David, Summer joined the kids.

"Ho! Ho!" David called, and the kids giggled. The tractor lurched into action with a roar of the engine, and Summer shouted, "Kids, hold on." But there weren't any sideboards on the wagon bed, so there was nothing for them to grab in an emergency.

David glanced over his shoulder. "Everybody still aboard?"

"Yes, but not any thanks to you. Watch what you're doing," Summer said severely.

David started singing "Jingle Bells" and the kids joined in the merry tune.

"Sing with us, Auntie," Nicole said.

David was traveling at a snail's pace. The wagon bed wasn't more than a foot off the ground and it probably wouldn't hurt if they did fall off, so she joined her soft contralto to the singing. In the middle of "Oh, what fun it is to ride," David suddenly hit the brakes, and his three passengers rolled off the wagon into a snowbank.

Timmy and Nicole shouted joyfully as they landed, but Summer's fall dislodged some snow that completely covered her head.

"Hey, I'm sorry, are you hurt?" David shouted, and he jumped off the tractor.

"We're all right," Nicole shrieked, "but Auntie is buried in the snow."

The force of the blow had stunned Summer momentarily, but she felt tiny hands clawing at the snow piled on her head. David knelt beside her and lifted her into his arms. Her face was plastered with snow, and she felt David's soft touch wiping away the moisture.

"Summer," he said, "speak to me. Are you all right?" His usually calm voice was rough with anxiety.

She started to open her eyes and assure him she was all right, but remembering the many times he'd pestered her with his dry wit, she decided to teach him a lesson. She moaned and went limp in his arms.

"Summer," he cried. "Don't tell me you're hurt!" His arms tightened possessively.

Touched by the concern in his voice and being so comfortable in his embrace, Summer's heart sang with delight. In spite of herself, she grinned and opened her eyes. David stared at her and burst out laughing.

"You mean you were only funning me!"

"Next time, watch how you drive!"

But her amusement suddenly diminished and excitement replaced it when a muscle quivered in David's jaw and he lowered his head. She struggled in his arms and her lips parted in surprise when he whispered her name in a silky tone she'd never heard him use before. Summer eagerly responded to the touch of his lips, and her arms went around his neck, molding her body into a closer embrace.

She had difficulty returning to reality when he lifted his head, whispering in her ear, "We've got an interested audience in case you've forgotten."

Her eyes snapped open to see Timmy and Nicole kneeling beside them, a glint of wonder in their eyes at this display of affection between their aunt and uncle. She and David had been so careful before not to exhibit their mutual attraction in front of the children.

Breathlessly, Summer said, "Let me go, David. I'm not hurt. What happened?"

He stood up and steadied her. "A deer ran in front of the tractor." In a teasing tone, he said to the kids, "It might have been Rudolph the Red-Nosed Reindeer, and I didn't want to hit it. Are you kids okay?" he asked.

Still wide-eyed at the adventure and its aftermath, Nicole and Timmy only nodded. David tried to catch Summer's eyes, but she didn't look at him as she helped the kids back on the wagon.

"I'll be more careful," David promised. "There might not be a convenient snowdrift the next time."

Timmy and Nicole huddled together, whispering, as he put the tractor into motion. Summer tried to ignore their words, but one comment did disturb her when Nicole murmured, "Just like Mommy and Daddy," and darted a quick look in Summer's direction.

The children had enough to threaten their security

without seeing the passionate display David and she had just exhibited. And Summer couldn't deal with it, either. She didn't want to become more closely tied to David than she was already, but these passionate encounters were occurring more and more frequently, and it was easy to see where they were heading. Although she seldom remembered her desire to leave The Crossroads and return to the corporate world, her ambition did surface occasionally. Increased emotional involvement with David would be a hindrance to that ambition.

David stopped the tractor near a grove of small evergreens, and the kids bolted through the trees, arguing over which one they should cut. Summer and David hurried after them.

"Remember," Summer cautioned, "there isn't enough room in the cabin for a big tree. We should have one that sits on the table."

"Here's a little one," Nicole said, stopping beside a tree that was over five feet tall.

"I meant a tree not much taller than you are," Summer said.

"Oh, Auntie, we want one bigger than that," Nicole protested.

After they'd searched the area and didn't find any small trees that suited the children, Summer threw up her hands in surrender.

"All right." She gave in graciously. "We'll move the desk out on the porch, cover it with plastic, and put the tree where the desk stands."

David handed a saw to Nicole and Timmy and showed them how to make a few indentations on the tree trunk with the saw before he took an axe and cut the tree. Summer stood to one side and watched her adopted family with gentle and contemplative eyes. David was wonderful with the children. He was patient with them and had stepped easily into the role of a father.

When they tied the tree on the wagon, there was hardly any room left, so David held Timmy on the tractor seat with him, and Nicole and Summer walked back to the cabin.

While David and the kids worked to secure the tree in the holder, Summer made toasted-cheese sandwiches, heated two cans of soup and washed several red apples.

Although the kids were excited and seemed happy as they trimmed the tree, Summer wondered if they were remembering the previous year when their parents were with them. Had she done enough to bring security and contentment to Timmy and Nicole?

Spring's tree decorations had once been used at the Weaver home in Ohio, and Summer reminisced on her childhood days as they worked. She'd let the kids choose a few special ornaments when they'd gone Christmas shopping the previous week, intending to start a tradition for them. At first Summer tried to organize the trimming so the tree would be artistic and decorative, but she finally gave up and let the kids do what they wanted to. The tree ended up being a hodgepodge of mismatched ornaments, jumbled tinsel and lopsided lights, but David and the children stood back and viewed their efforts with pleasure.

Rearranging two ornaments that she'd made in school out of clothespins, Nicole said, "I like it, don't you, Auntie?"

David's generous mouth trembled with unexpressed laughter, and Summer frowned at him. Deter-

mined not to lie, Summer said, "It's the most interesting Christmas tree I've ever seen."

Her answer seemed to satisfy the kids, and Timmy
said, "Can we put out some presents? Please!"

"Promise you won't be tearing the paper to peek
in the packages," Summer said.

"We won't," the children shouted in unison.

Summer looked at David to get his approval, and
he said, "I won't peek, either."

Summer shrugged her shoulders in a helpless gesture. "You're as bad as the kids. Go ahead and open
the box from Grandpa and Grandma Weaver."

Summer washed the dishes while David opened the
big carton and Timmy and Nicole pulled out a dozen
beautifully wrapped boxes and placed them under the
tree.

"I'll see that the kids get in bed," David said.

Summer was seated on the couch, her hands un-
consciously twisted together when David finally returned to the living room after trying for an hour to
get the children settled into bed.

"Too much excitement today. They're wound up
tonight. I hope they won't have nightmares."

"Timmy hasn't had a nightmare for several
weeks."

David glanced at his watch. "Almost eleven
o'clock. I'd better go, I suppose."

Summer didn't answer. He sat beside her and
placed his hand over hers. She cringed slightly, and
he knew this wasn't the time for a repeat of what had
happened earlier.

"Want to talk?" he asked.

"Oh, I don't know, David," she said in a resigned
tone. "When we moved to The Crossroads, I hoped

we'd become friends, but things are getting out of hand. There's no use ignoring what happened between us this afternoon.''

He lifted his hand and caressed the curve of her jaw. "I don't want to ignore it."

"We're together too much," she said, ignoring the import of his words. "But I don't think I can raise Timmy and Nicole without your help."

"It's only natural that we'd become close. I'm fond of you, Summer. I'm beginning to wonder just how fond! Do you suppose Spring and Bert had more than one reason for bringing us together?"

"I don't know! I don't even know who I am anymore. I'm losing my identity as Summer Weaver. I'm Auntie to the kids. I'm a big sister to the students. I'm not the same person I was a year ago, and it scares me."

"But I like the new Summer Weaver!"

A flash of humor crossed her face. "Didn't you like the old one?"

"Sure. But you've become more human, more alluring, more provocative. I wouldn't have kissed the old Summer like I did you this afternoon."

"Well, I haven't given up going back to New York, and I wonder what identity I'll have then. The present Summer wouldn't be happy in a corporate office. Will the former Summer surface when I'm back in New York, or is that Summer gone forever?"

"You'll always be yourself, even if your outlook on life changes. It's too late tonight for any philosophical discussions. I'll see you tomorrow."

He kissed her forehead and left the cabin. Even if her lips did say that they were spending too much time together, in her heart, Summer knew no matter how many other people were there, the cabin felt empty when David left it.

As Christmas Day neared, Summer overheard Timmy and Nicole talking about their parents. Nicole had little flights of fantasy when she pretended that her parents were coming, rather than her grandparents. And Timmy expected the Weaver grandparents whom he'd seen more often than David's folks. Although troubled about their illusions, Summer ignored her concerns, hoping the children would forget about missing Bert and Spring in the joy of Christmas.

David's parents arrived soon after noon on Christmas Eve. Patrick and Joyce Brown were both of medium height, and they had brown hair, brown eyes— people who wouldn't stand out in any crowd. But when you started talking with them, you realized how sincere they were in their Christian faith, and how their examples of morality, truth and honesty had produced sons like Bert and David. Summer had been so distressed during the time she'd seen the Browns at Bert and Spring's funeral that she hadn't passed more than a few words with them. Welcoming them to the cabin was almost like having strangers come, but she wanted to make them feel at home. This first Christmas after Bert's death would be a difficult holiday for them.

Still, she was a little nervous when David brought his parents to the house, wondering if they'd compare her to Spring and expect her to be like her sister.

Timmy and Nicole were standoffish at first, but they soon cuddled up to Patrick on the sofa and started talking about their school friends.

"Mrs. Brown," Summer said, "let me show you

the bedroom. The house is small, but I hope you'll be comfortable.''

"Don't fret about us. We came to visit Spring and Bert when they first moved in here. It's a nice little house, but small for a growing family.''

"Yes, it is,'' Summer agreed. "Daddy has offered to build another story so Timmy and Nicole can have separate rooms. But we'll wait and see how everything works out.''

"David said you're adjusting to the situation.''

"Yes, adjusting. David makes a good father, but I don't know how successful I am at mothering. It hasn't been easy for either of us.''

"We know it's been a great sacrifice for you, but God will help you if you'll trust Him for guidance.''

Summer didn't answer. Her faith was too new to understand God's will for her life, and how He'd brought her to this time and place.

When David and his father took the children sleighing, Summer was uneasy at being alone with David's mother. But Joyce was a comfortable woman to be around, and Summer soon felt at ease with her as they worked together to finish their Christmas Eve dinner.

Following the Weaver tradition, Summer had planned oyster stew, turkey sandwiches, raw vegetables and dip, fruit salad and an assortment of cookies for Christmas Eve. Joyce had brought fruit cake and a baked ham with pineapple sauce for dinner on Christmas Day.

"I hope you won't think I'm presumptive for bringing food. My fruit cake is a favorite of David's, and Patrick and I wanted to help out with your finances, so that's the reason for the ham. It wasn't that we thought you couldn't provide a meal.''

Summer's face broke into a wide smile. "You were wise to take precautions," she said. "I'm learning, but this is the first time I've ever been responsible for preparing the Christmas meals. I'd never cooked much, and I soon learned that children today don't eat the foods my mother provided for us. David is handy in a kitchen, so that's helped. He eats with us most of the time to give Timmy and Nicole a sense of family with a male influence, as well as mine."

After they ate supper, David and Patrick insisted on washing the dishes, and Summer decided David had followed the example set by his father. Later they sat around the fireplace while Patrick read the Christmas story from the book of Luke, then they sang carols and traditional songs.

Summer persuaded the children to go to bed so they could be up early to open packages, and after she returned to the living room, David said to his parents, "I think you'll be pleased to know that I've rededicated my life to Christ and that Summer accepted Him as her Savior a few days ago."

"That's wonderful news, David," Patrick said. "We've been praying for that to happen."

"It makes our work more meaningful," David said. "We knew we weren't qualified to take over a mission school, but we have a young chaplain who's taken care of the spiritual needs of the students."

"He's been a help to me, too," Summer said. "I had no biblical background to understand what was lacking in my life, but Curtis has counseled with me."

"Then both of you received the real gift of Christmas," Joyce said. "It will make a change in your lives."

David lingered until his parents went to their room, and he helped Summer set the table for breakfast.

"It will be pandemonium here in the morning," he said, "but we've made it easier for the children to face Christmas without their parents."

"I hope so."

David didn't want to leave this cozy home atmosphere and go to the dorm, but he'd loitered as long as he could. He put his arms around Summer and kissed her soft hair. She fit so well into his arms that he drew her closer.

"Merry Christmas, Summer."

She lifted her head, and their gazes held for a few electric moments before their lips met in a slow gentle caress. When he kissed the tip of her nose, she opened her eyes.

"Merry Christmas, David. The first Christmas we've spent together."

"Will it be the last?" he asked musingly, eagerness in his eyes.

"I don't know." But she threw him a kiss as he opened the door and left the cabin.

As she undressed for bed, Summer considered that their emotional life was becoming more complex. Where could they go from this point? She always felt comforted and cherished in David's arms. Could she be in love with him?

As David walked back to the dorm, his arms felt empty without Summer in them. The hours he spent with her and the children were satisfying, and the cabin home had the same atmosphere he'd always enjoyed as a child. But it disturbed him that Summer occasionally mentioned returning to New York. It seemed as if she still had to hold on to the past.

Chapter Fifteen

Summer made her bed on the sofa, but disturbed over her reaction to David's advances and wondering just what he meant by them, she couldn't go to sleep after she turned out the light. She was still awake when Timmy called, "Daddy! Daddy!"

Hoping to keep him from waking his grandparents, she jumped out of bed and sprinted down the hall in her bare feet. He wasn't calling out in his sleep. The child was awake, and his eyes were wide. She went inside the bedroom, closed the door and groped in the darkness until she found the light above his bed.

"I want my daddy."

"Uncle David just went home. He'll be back in the morning."

"No. I want my real daddy. He was supposed to come for Christmas. Why's he hiding from me?"

Nicole's feet were dangling over the side of her bed. "I told you, Timmy, that Daddy isn't hiding. He and Mommy are in Bolivia. They'll be back in a few months."

"But I want him *now!*" Timmy started kicking the blankets on his bed. "Now! Now!"

Oh, dear God, what can I do? Summer prayed. She couldn't leave the children and go for David. She could call Joyce or Patrick, but they were mourning enough already without having to deal with the children's fantasies and fears. No, she was on her own.

She sat on the bed beside Timmy, and he started pounding her legs. "Get away! Leave me alone. I want my daddy."

Summer caught his flailing arms. "Stop it!" She gathered him in her arms. "Nicole, come sit beside us."

Timmy started sobbing, and the sounds unnerved Summer. When Nicole sat on her other side, Summer took a blanket and covered the three of them, putting an arm around each child.

"Listen to me. Your parents are *not* in Bolivia. Nicole, you must not tell Timmy that again. Spring and Bert have gone to live with Jesus, and they aren't coming back. You must believe it."

"I don't think they'd go off and leave us forever," Nicole said stubbornly.

"You were at the farm when they were buried. You saw them in their caskets."

"That wasn't them—just somebody made up to look like them. Like we saw in a wax museum once," Nicole insisted.

"If they went to be with Jesus, why were they in them boxes?" Timmy wanted to know.

"I don't understand it very well," Summer admitted, "but we've got bodies and souls. The soul goes to Jesus, but the body is put in the ground. Someday the body and soul will be together again."

"Do you *really* believe that?" Nicole asked.

Summer hesitated, and the children watched her face intently. "Yes, I—I do," she stammered. "I don't understand it, but I believe it's true."

"I want them back," Timmy said.

"I miss them a lot, too, and wish they were with us, but it's not going to happen. We have to accept that. They asked your Uncle David and me to take care of you, and we're doing the best we can."

"You're doing all right," Nicole said, "but it helps to believe they've just gone away and will come back someday."

Summer wished she understood the basic Christian doctrine that everyone who died in Christ would someday live again, but even if she knew how to explain it, it would be too deep for the children.

"They can't return to us, but someday Jesus will take us to see them again."

"When?" Timmy asked.

"I don't know. Nobody knows except God."

"I don't understand," Nicole said.

"Neither do I. We're not expected to understand God's ways, just accept them," Summer said, realizing she'd just taken another giant step of faith in trusting God for the future.

Nicole sniffled, and Summer tightened her arm around the child.

"Can't you go to sleep now? We want to get up early in the morning to open presents. I'll stay with you."

Nicole refused to get back in her bed, so Summer said, "You stretch out beside Timmy, and I'll curl up at the foot of the bed until you're sleeping again."

* * *

The cabin was quiet when David walked up on the porch the next morning at six o'clock, but Summer heard him and opened the door.

"Ho! Ho! Ho!" he called, and she held up a cautious finger as he took off his coat and hung it in the closet.

"I don't think your parents are awake yet. I'm trying to get dinner underway before the children get up. What are you doing here so early?"

"I figured everybody would be up by now, ready to tear into their gifts," he said quietly, "and I didn't want to miss the fun. Besides, it was lonesome in that room all by myself."

Summer's mouth curved into a smile. "Okay, if you're looking for sympathy, I feel sorry for you. Last night I'd have gladly traded places with you."

She continued to crumble bread for dressing, and David stood beside her at the cabinet and started chopping celery and onions.

"What happened? I thought your voice sounded listless."

"I spent most of the night in the children's room, after learning that they still think their parents are coming back."

"Poor kids!" David said compassionately, and then he added, "And poor Summer for having to deal with it."

She explained what had happened and what she'd said to them. "I don't think I convinced them, but I did calm them and they went back to sleep."

"But you didn't."

"Perhaps I should have called your dad to talk to them, but your folks are having a difficult time themselves, so I toughed it out. Just when I think we're doing pretty well at this parenting business, something else comes up.''

''I have a feeling that real parents feel the same way. Rearing children is a big job.''

''But I'll admit I understand now why people choose to have children. I'm fond of Timmy and Nicole, and they aren't even mine. I find myself planning for their future, hardly ever thinking about my own aspirations. They've completely turned my life around, but I don't seem to mind.''

''Neither do I.'' The onion scent made David's eyes water, and sniffing, he turned to Summer. ''You're a pretty special person, Summer—at least, to me.'' He leaned toward her, but straightened when the hall door opened.

Summer turned and greeted Joyce and Patrick. ''Merry Christmas,'' she said.

Joyce came toward them and she put her arms around Summer. ''I heard Timmy cry out last night,'' she said, ''but I was too much a coward to go to him. I stood in the hallway and heard you talking with the children. Thank you, my dear.''

Patrick cleared his throat and took Summer's hand.

''But I didn't know what to say,'' Summer answered. ''I'm only beginning to understand the Christian faith myself so I can't explain it to anyone else.''

''You did as well as anyone could have,'' Joyce said. ''I believe God directed you. You're doing great with the children.''

Summer took David's hand. ''But not without David's help.''

''Let's have a prayer before the children get up,'' Patrick said, and the four of them joined hands while he prayed.

"Lord Jesus, we're sad this morning because our two loved ones aren't with us, but we know they're with You, and that makes us happy. We pray that You'll give David and Summer an extra portion of Your grace as they guide, protect and parent Nicole and Timmy. We ask, too, that David and Summer, following the path started by Bert and Spring here at The Crossroads, will find fulfillment for their own needs. Amen."

Sorrow was soon replaced by joy as Timmy and Nicole burst into the room, faces happy, as if the episode of the night before had never happened. Acting upon suggestions from Summer, her family had sent numerous books for the children, as well as warm clothing. David's parents had brought checkers, dominoes, and other table games. Summer welcomed these as good games for David and her to play with the kids.

Summer had vacillated for weeks before she finally bought David a red-and-gray pullover sweater. He was pleased with her choice, and he put it on at once.

She was amazed when she opened David's gift for her—a four-day bus tour to a resort hotel in Gatlinburg, Tennessee, usable any time during the next six months.

"Why, David! How thoughtful," she said. David's sensitiveness to her needs was one of the things that made him so special to her. After the first few weeks of frustration, she'd accepted the fact that she couldn't expect to have any time alone, but that didn't mean she didn't want to break away occasionally.

"Thank you very much. I do appreciate it," she said softly, and for a few tense seconds, his brown eyes met her blue ones. Summer forgot they weren't alone until Timmy crowded against her and demanded, "What'd you get? Must not have been much in a little box."

"Nice gifts don't always come in big packages," Summer said, and she lifted the gift certificate from the box. "This entitles me to a four-day vacation in the Smoky Mountains."

"Are we goin' too?" he asked.

"Nope," David answered. "The idea is for Summer to have a vacation from us."

"Gee whiz! Who's gonna look after us?"

"I'll do it," David said. "And we'll have pizza every meal."

"Oh, boy!" Timmy shouted.

Paper and ribbons littered the floor. Nicole was modeling a new dress, and David was placing batteries in a toy for Timmy when a knock sounded at the door. As fond as she'd grown of the students at The Crossroads, Summer was a bit annoyed that they'd come today. She had hoped for a family holiday.

David opened the door to Stonewall Blackburn. The mountaineer's black hat was white with frost and his whiskers bristled in the cold air.

"Come in, Stonewall," David invited.

"I'll step inside for a minute. Mighty cold out this mornin'." He touched the brim of his hat and nodded toward Patrick and Joyce. "Just come down with a gift for the children," he continued. He opened his coat and took out a puppy with a smooth white coat, black-and-tan patches and long drooping ears, and set it on the floor. The beagle yipped, waddled across the floor, grabbed a red ribbon in his mouth and tossed it upward.

"His name is Pete," Stonewall said.

Summer sensed three pairs of eyes staring at her. Two sets of beseeching juvenile eyes, and David's questioning gaze, displaying a bit of humor.

"Did you know about this?" she accused him.

His mouth twitched in amusement. "Not at all. I'm as surprised as you are. But I think it's a good idea. I like dogs."

"I know when I'm beaten," Summer said with a sigh. She turned to Stonewall. "Thank you, Mr. Blackburn. I'm sure the children will enjoy having a puppy."

Timmy and Nicole squealed and dived for the puppy. As they wrestled on the floor, Pete howled and ran away from them, dragging the red ribbon behind him.

"I want to hold him first," Nicole shouted.

Timmy shoved her away. "No, he's mine."

Smirking at David, Summer said, "You can settle the quarrel while I show Mr. Blackburn out."

"I'll build a house for the dog in a few days," Stonewall assured her.

"Please do," Summer said. "That way, the puppy can stay outside most of the time." She closed the door when Stonewall lumbered off the porch.

"He can sleep in our room," Timmy said, and Summer shook her head.

"No. Mr. Blackburn will build a house for Pete. Until then, we'll put him in a box here in the living room. Pete is a hound—he'll be happier outdoors, and so will I."

"Aw, gee," Timmy said and twisted his lips into a pout.

"Summer says the dog stays outdoors," David said

sternly. "Don't argue about it, or we'll give Pete back to Mr. Blackburn."

"All right," Nicole said, and Timmy's face retained its sullen look, but he didn't argue anymore.

Though his support made her days a lot easier, it irritated Summer that the kids would argue with her, but never with David.

Christmas night, David and his father took Nicole and Timmy for a walk while Summer and Joyce quietly washed the dirty dishes that had accumulated. Into the midst of this companionable silence, Joyce said, "Do you and David plan to get married?"

The dish Summer was washing dropped from her hands into the dishpan, splashing suds in every direction. For a full minute she was startled into silence, but her pulse quickened at the suggestion. "What gave you such an idea?"

Joyce laughed merrily. "Sorry to surprise you. It just appears to be the obvious solution. You seem quite compatible."

"Not always," Summer replied tersely. "We're wearing our company manners now."

"I'm sorry I mentioned it, but I wanted you to know that Patrick and I would approve if you should decide to marry. We appreciate what you've done for our grandchildren. We'd have taken them gladly, but I believe this arrangement is better, as Bert and Spring must have known it would be."

They planned the excursion to Biltmore on the day after Christmas and, fortunately, the weather cooperated. When Anita said, "I'm glad we're doing something special on our Christmas break, but what's so great about Biltmore?" David and Summer decided they needed to have an orientation before they started the day's journey. David circulated the news that everyone going to Biltmore should meet in the dining hall at eight o'clock.

All the students had gathered when Summer and her household arrived, and the noise in the cafeteria was deafening, but they settled down when David's shrill whistle sounded in the room.

"Today," he explained, "we're going to one of the most outstanding private homes in the United States. At the end of the nineteenth century, George Vanderbilt was responsible for the construction of Biltmore, a 250-room chateau near Asheville. It took hundreds of stonemasons and artisans six years to build the house, which was completed in 1895. We've arranged for a guide to take us through the large home, and I know you'll enjoy it. Be sure and follow directions and listen closely."

Summer drove the former Weaver van, and with David driving the school bus that belonged to the elementary school, they started off in a festive mood. Mayo had brought his new banjo, and he rode in Summer's van, leading the group in singing Christmas songs.

The weather was sunny, and they made the trip through Asheville and to Biltmore's private property without any trouble. Summer was caught up in the excited anticipation of the students, who stopped talking abruptly when they had their first view of the four-story stone house with the snow-covered Blue Ridge Mountains for a backdrop.

Anita moved to Summer's side. "You mean people actually live in that mansion!"

"I believe the owners live somewhere else," Summer answered, "and use this for special occasions only."

"I can't believe it."

David didn't have to caution the students about their behavior as they trailed behind the guide through the elaborately decorated home. In addition to the forty-foot-tall tree in the banquet hall, there must have been fifty other trees in the house, all decorated differently. It was a step back in time for the students as they saw the house as it had been a century ago.

After walking for three hours, they were ready for lunch by the time they finished their tour in the basement where Mr. Vanderbilt had provided a swimming pool, gymnasium and bowling alley for his family and guests.

Patrick bought lunch for everybody at the snack bar, and Summer took candid pictures of the group as they ate, intending to send them to her parents. Clara and Landon would be glad to know how she'd spent the Christmas present they'd sent her.

On the return trip, as they left Asheville behind them, Summer encouraged her passengers to talk about the day. "What impressed you the most?" she asked. "What did you like the best?"

"I liked the music room and the organ pipes in the banquet hall," Mayo said.

Others voiced their delight in the winter garden filled with orchids, tall palms and banana trees. One girl was impressed by the library with its numerous books.

Anita was sitting in the front seat beside Summer, and she didn't respond. "Didn't you have a good time, Anita?" Summer asked quietly, her words covered by the chattering students behind them.

Although Anita usually enjoyed a chance to go out in the van, she stared straight ahead with stony brown eyes.

"No, I didn't enjoy it," she said harshly. "I'd have been better off not to see the way rich people live."

"The Vanderbilts have always been generous with their money, giving large amounts to universities and other worthwhile civic projects."

"Makes no difference. They had no right to squander money on a house like that when people are in need. When I compare Biltmore to the house my mother and I lived in, I could scream. What kind of house does your family have?" She eyed Autumn belligerently.

Summer risked a glance at Anita's stormy eyes before she swung into a wide mountain curve. "Nothing to compare with Biltmore. My parents have a nice, comfortable home, but I don't think it's fair to resent people who have money. Today's trip wouldn't have been possible if my folks hadn't paid for it."

"I thought the school took care of it."

Summer shook her head, keeping her eyes on the road for they'd reached the mountain, and she was never comfortable driving over that route.

Anita's moody expression remained, so Summer asked, "How was your visit with the Blackburns?"

"All right, I guess. Hallie fixed a good dinner, and they had a package for me—a new sweater."

"That was nice of them."

"Yes, especially when I hardly ever get any new clothes." Anita managed a grin. "I'm glad you took us to Biltmore. I get cranky because I'm worried about what I can do when spring comes and I've finished my studies at The Crossroads."

Summer thought of her idea to take Anita with her to New York at the end of a year. Anita could help with the children while Summer worked, and perhaps go to school at night. With all of them gone, would David be lonely? He'd become a part of her life now. Would she be willing to leave him behind?

Chapter Sixteen

After the first of the year when school was again in session, David and Summer tried the first of their open house gatherings for The Crossroads students. They prepared chili soup, corn bread, raw vegetables with dip and brownies for dessert. After they'd eaten, the students competed vigorously in some of the table games Nicole and Timmy had gotten for Christmas. Mayo played his banjo and Curtis taught the students some new songs.

Considering the gathering a success, the next day, David and Summer tabulated the cost and tried to determine if they could make it a monthly function.

David sat on the side of her desk. Summer turned to the computer and opened the financial statement file. Pointing to the low balance, she grinned up at David.

"Big ideas, little money!"

"Yeah, that's true, but we're the only ones who know how hard up we really are. I vote to have the dinner every month."

"I agree with you. We'll have to cut corners some other way. Actually, I suppose it doesn't cost any more to buy food for them to eat in the cabin as in the cafeteria, and it's a lot more fun for the students."

Looking down at her intensely, David's forefinger traced the soft curve of her face from forehead to her jaw, and she grew warm when his hand came to rest on her shoulder. "You're making lots of people happy, including me."

Still sensitive to the thrill she experienced from his touch, Summer met his eyes with hers, and she suddenly realized how much David meant to her. He wore the red sweater she'd given him for Christmas, and the brilliant color emphasized his natural good looks and vitality.

"We do make a good team," she answered, and placed her hand over his as it rested on her shoulder.

"Sure do. We've done pretty well with this parenting thing and with the school administration, too."

David's hand closed over Summer's right shoulder and he pulled her upward into his arms. His brown eyes searched hers. "We never have any time by ourselves. Let's take Saturday off and go someplace—just the two of us. I can't even hold you in my arms, without expecting someone to barge in on us. We can take in a movie, have dinner or whatever you want to do."

As the weeks had passed, Summer had become increasingly aware of David's physical appeal, and she often resented the duties that kept them apart. After Christmas they'd agreed, in the interest of the children's emotional security, to repress their feelings and not to delve deeply into the mutual attraction they shared.

"It would be wonderful to have a day off. I'll see if Anita will help with the children. She's mature enough to make decisions if a crisis comes up. We'll decide what we want to do as we go along."

He kissed both her cheeks. "We'll have a great time. I've never forgotten that day we spent together in Ohio."

"Neither have I."

They left The Crossroads at ten o'clock and drove south though the national forest, bypassing the interstate, taking less-traveled roads. David drove slowly, stopping occasionally to enjoy the panoramic views of the mountains. They didn't talk a great deal, for David sensed that Summer preferred silence.

They continued easterly until they came to Chimney Rock and took the elevator to the top. With the foliage off most of the trees and a bright sun illuminating the lookout, they had a spectacular view of the terrain. The wind was raw and strong, and they didn't tarry long.

They circled back to Asheville, and David located a Victorian inn nestled in a two-acre wooded cove. The century-old house with its wraparound gingerbread porch reminded Summer of her home in Ohio. The dining room was cozy with a wood-burning fireplace, and they were shown to a window table that gave them a view of one of the majestic mountains surrounding Asheville.

They chose the luncheon speciality—hot salmon mousse with egg sauce, shoestring potatoes, peas and stuffed cucumber salad with hot rolls. For dessert they ordered blueberry turnovers served with pecan sauce.

When he finished his dessert, David asked the

waiter for coffee and ordered tea for Summer. He leaned back in his chair.

"Well, we've been at The Crossroads for over three months. We had a lot of doubts at first. How do you feel about the situation now?"

Summer squeezed a section of lemon into the steaming cup of tea. Laughing, she said, "Only three months! I feel as if I've spent half of my life buried in these mountains. That means it's only nine months until I go back to New York."

"Do you really believe, after a year at The Crossroads, that you'll want to go back to your life as it was before?"

"I don't suppose my life will ever be like it used to be, but I still wonder if Timmy and Nicole might become better adjusted adults if they don't live such a sheltered life as they do here. I'm not sure The Crossroads will prepare them to live in the real world. They may be too protected for their own good."

He shook his head. "Growing up in a big city isn't always good for kids, either."

"I'm sure Daddy would provide tuition so they can attend private schools where they'd get an excellent education. As a matter of fact, I've even thought of taking Anita with me. She's worried about what she can do when she graduates. She could watch the children while I'm at work, and she could attend school at night. I could finance that."

"Who'd do your work at The Crossroads?"

"I really haven't given any of this much thought. As you know, my roles as secretary, bookkeeper and mother don't leave me much time for thinking. I might be of more help to The Crossroads in New

York making a big salary and helping to support the work of the school.''

David refrained from saying, ''What about *us?*''

He enjoyed working with her, and the evenings in the cabin with her and the children were peaceful and memorable. After observing how she'd sacrificed her own desires for Timmy and Nicole, he wouldn't oppose her taking the children to New York, but how much would he like The Crossroads if Summer wasn't there?

Looking out the window to the mountains, David said, ''I've about decided to ask for a full-time appointment.''

''David!''

''It's been a slow process, but I've gradually been drawn back into the fellowship with God that I experienced when I was a boy. Since Christmas, I've been praying, talking to Curtis and reading the Bible. God has been dealing with me, and while I don't feel inclined to be a preacher like Bert was, I do think God is calling me to serve at The Crossroads. Preaching the Gospel is perhaps the primary goal of the school, but good administration also has its place in molding the lives of these young people. The weeks we've been here has been a crossroads for me, too. After seeing the needs of so many youth, I can never go back to the self-centered life I used to live.''

The other diners had already left the room, and the silence was pierced when a burning log crumpled, sparks snapped and drifted upward to the chimney. David carefully watched the play of emotions on Summer's face—surprise, indecision, resignation.

''Then you intend to stay here the rest of your life as Edna has done?''

"I don't know how long I'll stay. Right now, I can't see beyond the needs of these young people."

Her face wrinkled into worry lines, and David was sorry he'd brought up the subject. Things hadn't turned out as he'd expected. He'd suggested the day so they could concentrate on one another, and they'd spent the last two hours talking about their work at The Crossroads. Summer had been relaxed, and he shouldn't have distressed her.

"I'd like for you to stay with me," he said softly.

A host of confused thoughts and emotions disturbed her. It upset her that David was ready to commit to the work of their siblings and she wasn't. Did he want her to stay so their present relationship could continue or did he mean more than that? She became increasingly uneasy under his scrutiny and she looked away.

"I honestly believe it would be good for Timmy and Nicole to have the advantage of a more structured education, and I'd like to help Anita develop her musical talent." To her bewilderment, her voice broke slightly, and a hint of uncertainty crept into her expression. "But when I get that far in my planning, a red flag takes over my thoughts, and your name is written all over it."

The waiter hovered with their check, and David waved him away.

"It isn't easy for me to let go of a lifetime goal. I came here to fulfill Spring's dream, but I didn't expect to give up everything I'd ever wanted. Although in my mind, I believe I'll have to do it, I haven't come to the point when I can mark off my personal aspirations."

He reached for her hand. "I shouldn't have said

anything. Let's forget the past and the future and just enjoy the rest of the afternoon. What do you want to do now?"

Relieved that she didn't have to give an immediate answer to his invitation to stay with him, Summer said, "There are lots of antique stores in Asheville. Let's browse in those for an hour or so. I don't suppose I'll buy anything, but it's interesting for me to find items like we have on the farm and see how much they're worth."

They spent a couple of hours wandering around the city hand in hand, buying nothing except an armload of children's books in a used bookstore. When they left Asheville, David tugged on Summer's hand and she moved closer to him.

"Have fun?"

She laid her head on his shoulder. "It's been a wonderful day. I'd rather not go back to meager bank accounts, fussing children, hurting youth and a howling pup." She sighed. "But I'd soon get tired of loafing."

"I'm really proud of you and the way you've taken over difficult tasks and made them look easy. Deep down, I know you don't want to be at The Crossroads, but you conceal it from others."

"But it bothers me, David, that I don't do it with any real compassion for them. You're dedicated to what you're doing, but I'm like my mother, I suppose. She did her duty no matter how painful it was, not because she wanted to, but because it was expected of her."

"For whatever reason, you're doing great."

A mile from The Crossroads, David pulled to the

side of the road. He didn't intend to let the day end on a somber note.

"There's only one other thing I need to make this a perfect day. Do you mind?" David put his arms around Summer and held her closely for a few minutes. Then he gently nudged her head backward with his chin, and his brown eyes gleamed with an invitation when he kissed her.

Summer closed her eyes, unable to hold his gaze any longer. His caresses lasted a long time. When he released her and moved away, she said quietly, "That made it a perfect day for me, too."

When she was in David's embrace, she never doubted that she wanted to stay with him.

"We'd better go on now," David said. "The kids will be looking for us."

"And don't forget Pete will be, too."

Although at first Summer could see nothing amusing about the fact that the puppy had become her shadow, she'd finally accepted that as she had the other changes in her life. In spite of the fine doghouse that Stonewall had built, Pete refused to live in it. If they put him outside, he'd stand at the door and howl all night long until, in desperation, Summer would get up and let him in the house. Instead of going to the children's bedroom, where he'd have been received with open arms, Pete curled up beside Summer's bed, and a few times when she'd awakened, he'd been lying at her feet.

Pete played with the kids, but he gave Summer his full devotion. Summer knew she was stuck with the animal, and she already dreaded having a full-grown hound in the crowded cabin. Still, she was glad she'd allowed the kids to have the dog, for he gave them lots of pleasure.

Although the children had seemingly gotten over their grief, Timmy still awakened at night calling for his parents, and Nicole occasionally had flights of fancy when she imagined her parents were returning in a few months. Acting on Curtis's advice, David and Summer talked to the children about their parents, trying to keep their memory alive in a healthy way. She hung the picture collage from her New York apartment, showing the Weaver sisters during various stages of their childhood. Summer told them about their mother and her childhood growing up in Ohio, of how the three Weaver girls and the Belgian horses had participated in parades and horse shows throughout the Midwest.

The snowy, cold weather persisted for weeks after Christmas, and no one stayed outside for long. David and Summer hardly had a moment of privacy. He'd come to terms with his attraction for Summer, and knew that he loved her, but with so many people around all the time, he couldn't find the time to tell her so.

One night when Anita and a couple of the boys came to watch television, David took matters into his hands, and said, "I want to go into town and mail a letter. Can you watch Timmy and Nicole for a little while, so Summer can go with me?"

"Sure thing, David," Anita said with a saucy look. "Have fun!"

As they walked toward the parking lot, Summer said teasingly, "What letter did you want to mail?"

"I don't know, but I'll find something in the office

that ought to be mailed. A house full of teenagers was more than I could cope with tonight.''

"I thought you were the one who liked to be around people."

"I still do, but sometimes it's nice to limit the company to one person."

"I feel flattered," she said playfully, feeling carefree and excited. She'd missed being alone with David, too.

A mile from The Crossroads, David slowed the car and stopped in the middle of the road. There was seldom any traffic on the mountain at night. He stretched out his hand to her and she moved closer to him. Putting his arm around her waist, he gave her an affectionate squeeze.

"I hope you didn't mind my bringing you on a needless errand, but I thought the nightly crowds have been getting on your nerves."

She stirred uneasily in his embrace. "When Timmy and Nicole are fighting, when Timmy is sick or having nightmares and I feel so inadequate to deal with him, when that little cabin, which isn't a whole lot bigger than my bedroom at the farm, is overrun by noisy teenagers, and I have no privacy anywhere, I wonder how I'll stand it another day. But when I see Anita smile or hear Mayo play his banjo and sing, 'My God is an Awesome God,' I can't imagine living anywhere else. Then I feel as if we're actually making a difference in their lives."

"The lack of privacy doesn't bother me like it does you for our house was small, and we had lots of cousins and friends around all the time. Spending ten years in the Air Force didn't give me much privacy, either.''

"You'd probably perish if you were abandoned on a desert island and couldn't talk to anyone. I think I'd thrive on the solitude."

"You'll have a chance to find out when you take that vacation trip to the Smoky Mountains. Have you decided when you'll go?"

"Sometime in April, I think. The next time I'm in Asheville, I'll go to the travel agency and schedule the tour, then I can arrange my office work to suit that time frame. I'll have to make some provision for Timmy and Nicole, for you shouldn't have to shoulder that responsibility since you'll be doing my office work."

"Anita will help with the children during the day, and I'll stay in the cabin at night. You'll only be gone a few days."

He inhaled the fragrance of her hair and planted a kiss on the ear that nestled against him. "In spite of our differences, we've made a good team. Do you..." He hesitated, hardly knowing how to speak, but wanting to know how she felt. "Would you consider making this a permanent arrangement?"

What a dumb way to ask a woman if she wants to marry you! David thought, inwardly groaning at his ineptitude. Was he so afraid that Summer would reject him that he couldn't come right out and tell her what his heart felt? No wonder she misunderstood him!

"We haven't been here six months yet," she said. "I still think it's best to reserve our decision until the end of our first year. Now it feels right to be here, but we're talking about a lifetime. I don't want to make any mistakes."

"But I wasn't referring to..."

"There's a car coming up the mountain," Summer

said, and the intimate moment was broken. Sighing, David continued their trip into Mountain Glen. They went into a café for coffee and lingered almost an hour before they drove back to The Crossroads.

David had hoped to get Summer to express her feelings for him, but she had her guard up now, and he knew tonight wasn't the time to press her for a commitment.

"I'll walk with you to the cabin to be sure everything is all right before I turn in." David took her arm and before they reached the cabin, he dropped a soft kiss on her lips.

David opened the door, Pete barked and ran to Summer and wound himself around her feet. The boys had gone, and Anita was watching television.

"Everything all right?" David asked.

"I put the kids to bed, heard their prayers 'n' everything," Anita said. "Now, I've got to scat. I have an English test tomorrow. I'll walk back with you, David."

After she got into bed, Summer reflected on their evening. She hadn't misunderstood David's question about becoming a permanent team. But she wasn't ready to deal with a decision about marriage. Her admiration for him was growing, but did she love him? She often thought her feeling for him was love, but did she love him enough for marriage? After being a loner all her life, could she ever give herself completely to anyone?

It had been so long since she'd gone any place alone that Summer felt conspicuous when she boarded the bus in Asheville. Without a traveling companion, Summer was asked to take a seat behind the driver which was a bit crowded for two people. She was glad to sit alone for she didn't want to talk to anyone. She kept remembering her departure from The Crossroads. Both Timmy and Nicole had cried and clung to her when she left, and Pete had barked and raced after the car until she sped up and left him behind.

"What if you don't come back like our other Mommy?" Nicole cried, and Timmy begged, "Don't go. I'll miss you."

The students from The Crossroads had grouped outside to watch her early-morning departure, and Summer's eyes misted over.

"Maybe I'd better not go," she'd said quietly to David, who stood beside the open car door.

He drew Timmy and Nicole away from her. "Listen, kids. Summer's going to unwrap the gift I gave her for Christmas. You wouldn't want to have a gift you'd never opened, would you? Be good now. I'll look after you while she's gone. She'll be home in four days."

"Promise you'll come back," Timmy said.

Summer darted a quick glance at David and lines of concern appeared between her eyes. She thought of the deaths of Bert and Spring. They'd intended to return to The Crossroads, too. She'd kept her promise to her sister, but how could she make another promise she might not be able to keep?

"God will take care of your Auntie," David said to the kids. "Go on, Summer. They'll be all right."

The memory of their worried faces had been in her mind all the way down the mountain. She'd been touched by the children's crying—so much that she hadn't wanted to leave them.

The first stop was at Cherokee, North Carolina, located on the Cherokee reservation, where the tourists viewed a Native American village as it would have looked in the eighteenth century. In the craft shop, Summer bought two dolls in traditional costumes for Nicole and Timmy.

After lunch, the bus continued across the steep mountain road into Tennessee to the inn where they would stay for two nights. The inn was located on a wooded mountainside overlooking downtown Gatlinburg. Summer's room had a private balcony, and before going to dinner, she sat outside and enjoyed the cold air. She heard the sound of traffic in the town below, but otherwise, all was quiet. How long had it been since she'd had any peace and quiet? In the cabin, even after the children were in bed, there was sound as the children turned in bed or Pete snored noisily at the foot of her bed. And Summer was always listening for Timmy's nightmares. Well, she had the solitude she'd been wanting. Nothing would disturb her tonight.

She glanced at her watch—seven o'clock. Supper would be over in the cabin, Timmy and Nicole would be vying for a coveted place on the floor in front of the television and Mayo and Skipper would be coming to watch the game shows. And David? What would he be doing? Probably helping Anita clear away the supper dishes. With a sigh, Summer went into her room to change her clothes before dinner. She took a framed photo from her suitcase and set it on the table by her bed. David's mother had taken the picture of Summer and David and the children on Christmas Day. Summer hadn't paid much attention to the framed photo when she was at The Crossroads, but when she'd packed her suitcase, she'd included the picture.

The next morning, in small buses, the group took a tour of the national park, and everyone cheered when a couple of black bears ran across the road in front of them. The guide said they were fortunate as these were the first bears he'd seen this spring. In the afternoon, they took a tour of Christus Gardens, enjoying the realistic scenes portraying the life of Christ, as well as the colorful floral settings.

The pace was leisurely, with long lunch stops and bountiful dinners at good restaurants. Normally, the unhurried pace would have suited Summer's tastes, but she'd become accustomed to the hectic activities at The Crossroads, and the days passed slowly for her. On the day before their return home, the tourists visited shops in Pigeon Forge.

She bought perfume for Anita, a doll for Nicole, a cuddly black bear for Timmy, a brown tie that reminded her of David's eyes and even a plastic bone for Pete. Since she couldn't afford to buy anything individually for the rest of the students, she settled for two large cans of cookies.

The tour included a farewell meal at a large steakhouse, where the guests were entertained by a violinist. Summer was sorry when they boarded the bus to go back to the inn to face another night in an empty room.

She undressed and put on a nightgown and robe. She sat on the side of the bed and picked up the photo of her family. *Her family!* Had she started thinking of them as her family? She ran her fingers over the image of Timmy's fair complexion, dwelling a moment on his small, rounded nose. Imaginatively, she smoothed back Nicole's hair that was always falling over her forehead. Her hands caressed David's features. She lifted the picture and kissed each of the smiling faces before her.

She laid the picture beside her pillow as she got into bed and turned out the light. This trip hadn't turned out at all as she'd expected it to. David had purchased the tour so she could have a few days of the solitude she'd liked. Had he suspected how the trip would affect her?

She had been lonely for three days. She could have made friends with other tour members, but it wasn't just anyone's companionship she craved. She wanted David and Nicole and Timmy. Had these three people wrapped themselves around her heart and emotions until she needed them to have a complete life? It was a frightening thought. Would she ever be content to be alone again?

School was being dismissed for the day when Summer drove into the compound parking lot. Remembering how disturbed she had been when she'd seen the compound for the first time, she couldn't believe how good the area looked to her today. She turned off the engine and eagerly stepped out of the car.

A shout reached her ears and she turned to see Timmy running down the steps of the elementary school. He should have had his coat on, but without scolding, she reached down for him and swung him into her arms.

"Auntie!" he shouted. "We've missed you."

His welcome had alerted the area, and several of The Crossroads' students rushed into the parking lot and gathered around her. Nicole pushed her way through the students and put her arms around Summer's knees. Summer set Timmy on the ground and hugged his sister.

Summer was overwhelmed by the warm homecoming, but something was missing. She looked around. David? Where was David? Then he appeared at her side.

"Hey," he said, "it's my turn for a hug." He pulled her close in a possessive gesture, and under cover of the general hubbub, whispered for her ears alone, "It's not the same when you're gone."

Timmy tugged on her hand. "Let's go home. I want you to fix supper. Uncle David and Anita don't know how to cook."

She exchanged amused glances with David, remembering a few months ago when Timmy hadn't liked *her* cooking.

"And Pete wants to see you, too. He's been whining ever since you left," Nicole said.

"Wait until I get my things out of the car." She put the two tins of cookies in the hands of Mayo, thinking he was the most likely student to see that the sweets were equally shared. David picked up her suitcase, and Timmy and Nicole carried some of her packages as they walked along the narrow path that would take them home. Home! Had this place really become home to her?

Pete was chained to his house to keep him from running off to look for Summer. She reached down and unchained him, and he ran into the house before the rest of them.

The children were so excited to have her home, and pleased over the gifts she'd brought that she had difficulty getting them settled for the night. It was after ten o'clock before Summer and David had the cabin's living area to themselves, and they sat together on the sofa.

"Thanks for the Christmas gift in April," Summer said. "It was a well-planned tour. My room at the inn was a beautiful place, and all of the meals were fabulous."

She became silent, and David watched her face closely as she talked about the places she'd seen.

"I learned a lot of things on this trip that surprised me, things I'm not sure I wanted to learn."

Gathering her into his arms, David murmured, "Tell me."

She pushed back a strand of wayward hair from David's forehead. "I had the solitude I've been thinking about for the past six months. I sat alone on the bus. I roomed alone. I didn't make any friends. Most everyone had a companion, and while several people asked me to join them, it didn't appeal to me. And I was lonely, David. I kept thinking how much more fun I'd have if you and the kids were with me."

"Maybe we've become a habit with you."

She continued as if she hadn't heard him. "So I'll have to reassess my priorities. I apparently can't be satisfied with my life as it used to be. Were Spring and Bert right? Am I finding at The Crossroads what I've been searching for? For months I've worried that I've been doing the things I do because I thought it was my duty. I know now that *love* not *duty* has motivated me. It's frightening not to be the person you used to be. I hardly know who I am anymore."

David's embrace tightened. "I know who you are—the most captivating woman I've ever known. This place has been like a prison while you were gone. The minute you get back, I'm enthusiastic about my work again.''

He kissed her cheek, but Summer's thoughts were still on the change in her attitude. ''And while the bus made its way toward Asheville, I kept thinking, 'I'm going home.' Has The Crossroads really become my home?''

''I learned something while you were gone, too. I'm not satisfied at The Crossroads unless you're here.''

''So it looks as if our decision is becoming more complex rather than easier.''

David agreed, kissing the soft hair resting on his shoulder. ''I'll have to go back to the dorm now, but I'd much prefer to stay here.''

Summer let his remark go without an answer. She knew what David meant, but she wasn't ready to deal with anything *that* complex right now.

Chapter Seventeen

The rest of April passed rapidly, and graduation ceremonies were planned for the five seniors. To Anita's relief, David received permission from the mission board for her to work at The Crossroads for a year with a small income until they could make arrangements for her to attend college.

The mission board had also arranged for David to take a week's tour to churches in Virginia and North Carolina during the first week in May, to report on the work at The Crossroads and to enlist their support for future projects. The monthly newsletters had paved the way for the requests that he intended to make—new kitchen equipment, a computer lab, a gymnasium, office equipment and a piano.

"Do you actually think you'll get commitments for all of that?" Edna asked as they sat in their monthly staff meeting the last week in April.

"No," David said, smiling. "But we sure won't get it if we don't ask. I'm also going to ask the board to approve an open house at the beginning of the school year, so people can see what we're doing.''

As Summer listened to David's enthusiastic plans, she knew he'd found his place. He intended to stay at The Crossroads. The next decision was up to her. Would she stay with him? If so, in what role?

She'd missed part of the conversation while she'd been woolgathering, but she paid attention when David said, "I've considered taking Mayo and Skipper with me. The boys sing well together, and if people hear a demonstration of Mayo's talent on the piano, perhaps they'll be more generous. I've seen a big change in attitude and spiritual growth in those boys in the seven months I've been here. They'll be a good advertisement for the school.''

"You certainly have my permission,'' Edna said. She turned to Summer, "Can you manage the office alone while David is gone? We can probably get a volunteer to come in and help.''

Summer didn't want David to leave, but not because of the extra work she'd have to do. "I'll manage all right,'' she said. "Anita is handy with the copier and other equipment, so I'll call on her if I need any extra help.''

They closed the office when the meeting ended, and David walked back to the cabin with Summer.

"So this time I'm going and you're staying behind. Do you realize that, except for the few days you went on your tour, we've been together every day since the first week in October?''

"I'm going to miss you, but a few days of separation might be good for us—maybe give us a new perspective on...on things. I depend on you too much.

This will be a good time to see if I can handle the household by myself."

David left early the next morning, with the whole Crossroads student body on hand to see him off. Skipper's wide smile lit his features as he anticipated the journey before him. Mayo's expression seldom betrayed his inner feelings, but as he carefully stored his banjo in the back of the van, Summer noted a gleam of excitement in his eyes.

Summer and David had said their goodbyes before he left the cabin last night. A warm glow colored her face and her mind burned as she remembered the depth of their ardor. She was embarrassed in David's presence this morning, wondering just how much her response had revealed to him.

David bent to kiss Nicole and Timmy on their foreheads, squeezed Summer's hand, and stepped into the van that moved rapidly out of the parking lot to the concerted cheers of the students.

Skipper stuck his head out the window. "See you next Monday," he shouted.

Monday seemed a long way off, Summer thought as she watched Timmy and Nicole climb the steps to the elementary school, and she turned toward an empty office.

Mindful of their limited budget, David didn't telephone until Wednesday morning. Summer was pleased to report that all was well.

When the auditor arrived at the office early the next morning, Thursday started out on a sour note. She spent the entire day providing files for him, and although everything was in order, Summer was edgy, fearful that she hadn't kept the financial records to suit him. The man didn't leave until four o'clock, and

by that time Timmy and Nicole would have been at
home for almost an hour. She never left them alone
in the cabin, and she was anxious to get home.

Nicole was seated at the kitchen table doing her
homework.

Summer kissed her, asking, "Where's Timmy?"

"Outdoors playing with Pete, I reckon," Nicole
said.

"I didn't see Pete or Timmy. I'd better check on
them."

After calling for Timmy several times without any
response, Summer stuck her head in the door. "I'll
go back to the compound and look for him," she said
to Nicole. "Don't you disappear while I'm gone."

Engrossed in her homework, Nicole nodded her
head.

Summer wasn't much alarmed because Timmy
liked the playground equipment, but she didn't see
him or the dog with the other children. Outside the
administration building, she met Stonewall Blackburn, hobbling along with the aid of a heavy walking
stick.

"What's happened to you?" she said.

"I was fixing the siding on the cabin, and hit my
knee with a hammer," he said. "Can't hardly walk."

"I'm sorry about that. Have you seen Timmy? He's
not at the cabin, and I don't see him around here. He
was playing with Pete the last time Nicole saw him."

"Nope! I ain't seen the boy, but he might have
followed the hound into the woods. Pete's big enough
to want to hunt. After that rain last night, if he took
one of the trails, I ought to be able to find some
tracks. I'll walk back with you."

"Oh, you shouldn't do that, not with a sore leg," Summer protested.

Heading toward the cabin, Stonewall said, "It's good for a sore joint to exercise it—I'll go see what I can find."

Summer wanted to rush ahead, but she slowed her pace to match Stonewall's labored steps. If there were any signs to Timmy's disappearance, Stonewall could spot them easier than she could.

When they entered the glade, she went first to the overlook—she'd always feared one of the children might fall down that mountain. She tried to remember what Timmy had worn today. She was sure he had on his blue jacket, so that would be easy to see if he and Pete were in sight, but there wasn't a sign of either of them.

She joined Stonewall at the trail head, and he pointed to tracks in the muddy spot where the path entered the national forest.

"He's gone that way," Stonewall said, "and the dog was in front of him. Probably Pete ran away, and Timmy went after him."

The spring foliage wasn't full-leafed yet, and Summer walked along the trail a short way, hoping to see the boy.

"Timmy! Timmy!" she called several times, but he didn't answer. She went back to Stonewall.

"I'll go after him as soon as I let Edna know what's happened and get Anita to stay with Nicole. I'm worried."

Stonewall thumped her on the shoulder with his beefy hand.

"Now, missy, no need to worry. It's a long time

'til dark. Pete will head for home soon, and the boy will be along.''

Summer shook her head. "I'll go look for him."

"Sorry I can't help, but this leg wouldn't hold me up for long."

"Thank you. It's my responsibility. Like you said, he'll probably come home on his own, but I'll feel better if I'm doing something."

"You go on—don't wait for me."

Summer stopped in the cabin. "Nicole, he's gone into the woods, and I'm going to find him. You come with me, and I'll see if Anita can look after you until I get back."

Nicole started to protest, but perhaps sensing Summer's worry, she closed her book and came to the door. As they hurried along the path, Nicole said, "Just like that mean little boy to pull something like this. He ought to have a spanking."

Summer didn't answer, and Nicole said, "I wish Uncle David was here."

"Yes, so do I." But David wasn't here. Skipper and Mayo would have been helpful because they spent a lot of time together in the woods, but they were gone, too. Summer knew she was on her own.

Edna was in her office, and Summer explained her anxiety.

Edna locked her office. "Let's check in the kitchen. Anita will be helping with supper, but I can take over so she can look after Nicole."

"I think I should go with you," Anita said when they reached the kitchen. "You might need some help, and I know the forest trails pretty well."

"She's right, Summer," Edna agreed. "You shouldn't go alone. Nicole can stay with me."

Nicole started crying. "Don't leave me, Auntie. Let me go with you. I'm afraid."

Summer knelt and hugged her. "I don't know how long it will take to find Timmy, and you'd get tired. It will help the most if you stay with Edna."

Nicole swallowed a big sob and said, "Okay. I hope Timmy's not hurt."

"I'll get my heavy shoes, change into jeans and meet you at the cabin as quick as I can," Anita said.

By the time Anita got there, Summer had put a first-aid kit, health bars, water and some juice in a backpack. She picked up the big lantern and checked the batteries. She pulled on a heavy jacket, for the temperature was dropping steadily.

"What are your plans?" Anita asked as they started up the trail, Summer in the lead.

"I haven't had time to make any. We can follow his tracks as long as we can see them, then I'll start calling. Pete usually comes to me when I call, and he can lead us to Timmy."

"If he is lost, he'd be scared by now, and probably crying."

After they'd walked for over an hour, the tracks ended on a rocky point where the trail forked.

"Now what?" Anita said.

Summer shook her head. "I don't know." Looking upward, she prayed, "God, I don't have a clue to what I should do. You know where Timmy is—guide me."

She paused, still not sure which way to go, but Anita said, "I think I hear a dog barking that way." She pointed to the left.

Summer didn't hear the dog, but she turned left. "That's good enough for me. It's going to get dark in a few hours, and we've got to find him before that. I didn't think of this before we left, but we should have notified the forest rangers. I thought we'd find him long before now. Maybe Edna will think to notify them. They may have to rescue all three of us.''

"Oh, I'm not lost," Anita assured her. "I can find my way back home, but I'd rather do it before dark."

Summer soon heard barking, and she was sure it was Pete. She called, and soon Pete came scuttling toward them through the woods, and when he saw them, he started back the way he'd come, still barking. Summer broke into a run, with Anita at her heels. They caught up with Pete, standing at the edge of a rock cliff, barking and looking downward.

"Careful," Summer warned Anita as she dropped to her knees and crawled to the edge. A spot of blue several feet below showed where Timmy had fallen.

"Timmy!" she called. Pete was still barking, and she said, "Anita, try to keep the dog quiet."

She called several times, and when Timmy didn't respond, she said, "I'll have to go down there."

"But how?" Anita asked. "You can't go down this cliff."

"No, but if I backtrack a little, I can go around the side of the mountain. I'll have to hurry before it's completely dark. If I get into trouble, you go back to the compound and bring help."

Fear showed in Anita's eyes, but she said, "You'll be all right. But I oughta warn you—the park rangers have told us to stay away from cliffs like this after the snakes start crawling. They might have come out those warm days we had last week. So be careful."

Summer would have preferred that Anita hadn't divulged that information, but she steeled her mind against the danger she'd find at the foot of the cliff. Clinging to trees for support, and sliding on her rear down the steepest places, Summer finally reached the level where Timmy lay. Fearing what she'd find, she rushed to him and dropped to her knees.

From above, Anita called, "How is he?"

"He's alive, thank God." Summer touched Timmy's warm face and monitored his erratic pulse.

"Timmy," she said, taking him by the arm. He winced, but he opened his eyes.

"I'm hurt, Auntie," he said.

"Hurt where?"

"Arm?"

When she touched his left arm, Timmy groaned, but he didn't flinch when her hands moved over the rest of his body.

Putting her hand behind his back, she said, "Try to stand up. I have to take you back to the cabin before it gets dark."

Crying, Timmy said, "It's all Pete's fault. He runned away, and I was trying to catch him."

"Stand up, Timmy," she insisted, but when Summer pulled him upward, he fainted.

Calling on God for help, Summer lifted Timmy into her arms. Timmy wasn't a big boy, but he felt heavy to Summer as she started carrying him around the mountainside.

"Anita," she called. "If you'll come down and help put him on my back, I think I can carry him up the hill. His arm is broken."

While Anita scampered down the hill, Summer laid Timmy back on the ground, and removed her coat. She reached in the backpack, found a knife, and started cutting the coat into wide strips. Anita arrived breathless.

"Why are you doing that?"

"He keeps fainting, and we'll have to tie him on my back."

"Could we take turns carrying him?"

"Maybe. But let's try it this way first."

They made a harness out of the heaviest parts of the fabric and fit it around Timmy before they lifted him upward. He regained consciousness and started sobbing.

"Timmy, listen to me," Summer said. "Try to stay awake and hold on to me with your right hand. Anita, if you'll support him until we get to the trail, I can carry him, but I'll need my hands to hold the trees for leverage as I climb up the hill."

"Once we hit the trail, it will be mostly downhill."

"Are you mad at me, Auntie?" Timmy whispered.

"I'm not mad. I love you."

"I love you, too."

"Hang on," Summer said, starting up the incline, pulling muscles in her back and legs she didn't even know she had. She staggered and gasped for breath when she reached the trail.

"Here," Anita said, grabbing her arm. "Drink some of this juice."

"Thanks," Summer whispered. "Try to get Timmy to drink some water or juice."

After resting a short time, Summer started out. An hour before they reached The Crossroads, darkness surrounded them, and Anita walked behind her, shining the lantern light on the trail. Summer bypassed the cabin, saying to Anita, "Will you tie Pete up and then come help put Timmy in the car? I've got to take him to the hospital right away.''

Edna must have been watching, for she hurried to the car, with Nicole running beside her.

"Is he hurt?" Nicole asked. She ran over to Timmy and patted him on the sore arm. "Me and Miss Edna have been praying."

"He has a broken arm, and I hope that's all," Summer said. "I'll have to take him to the doctor." Looking at Edna, she continued, "Is it all right for Anita to go with me?"

"Certainly. I would go, but with you and David both gone, I should be here."

"Anita can cushion his head on her lap. He's hurting a lot."

"Maybe we should call an ambulance?"

"I can be at the hospital before they'd make it up the mountain, and after the way we jostled him around getting him out of the woods, a ride in the car won't hurt him anymore."

"I'll be praying for you," Edna said, taking Nicole by the hand and leading her inside the building.

Chapter Eighteen

As she started down the steep mountain, Summer said, "Thanks, Anita, for the way you've stood by tonight. I couldn't have handled it without you. Every day, I realize how much I need other people in my life."

Anita's voice broke a little as she answered, "I'm glad I can help somebody. My life has seemed worthless for several years, but coming to The Crossroads was the best thing that ever happened to me. Maybe I *can* amount to something."

"You amount to something already. You've been a friend to me."

Summer detected a sniff from the back seat. "I want to say what I think of you, too. I've looked at those pictures in the cabin that show you and your sisters, the big house you lived in and the nice farm. You've said enough for me to know that your parents have lots of money. Yet, you've given all of that up to come here to The Crossroads to help kids like me and Skipper and Mayo—kids that don't have anyone else to love them. That takes a lot of love, Summer.''

Now there was sniffing in the front seat as Anita continued. ''Last Sunday, Curtis read a Bible verse when Jesus said, 'Whatever you did for one of the least of these, you did for me.' While he talked, I thought of you and David. Thanks.''

Summer had to keep blinking back the tears so she wouldn't run off the road. Through Anita's words, Jesus Himself seemed to be approving what she and David were doing.

They didn't have to wait long in the emergency room before Timmy was taken in for X rays.

''Don't leave me, Auntie,'' he begged.

''I'm going to stay with you.''

The X rays showed a clean break, which would heal without any damage to his arm. ''But we do want to keep him overnight for observation,'' the doctor said. ''We can't see that he's hurt elsewhere, but we want to be sure.''

It was almost one o'clock before Timmy was moved to a room. Summer asked a nurse to bring a cot for Anita, but she herself sat by Timmy's bed, holding his hand, monitoring his breathing. Thanking God that Timmy was going to be all right, Summer's mind turned to the time she'd sat beside Spring's bed and watched her die. What a lot of changes had occurred in her life since then.

Although she'd been unhappy with the role Spring had forced on her, she realized now that she might never have known what it was to love if Spring hadn't appointed her guardian of Nicole and Timmy. She might have lived her life without loving David and the children. And she did love David—she'd known since she'd taken the bus tour, but she hadn't been able to tell him.

She'd allayed a lot of fears since she'd started out to find Timmy several hours ago. Summer had never driven down the mountain in the dark, but she hadn't even thought about the danger tonight. She hadn't had David or her parents tonight, yet she'd made decisions and carried them out. She'd depended upon God and her own resourcefulness. She wouldn't doubt again that she could be independent, but she'd also found out how much she needed the companionship of others.

As she sat watching Timmy's even breathing, Summer made a commitment to The Crossroads. She'd never be satisfied in a New York office after the experiences she'd had helping others. She smiled when she realized that she loved David as much as her sisters had loved the men they'd chosen. Now she understood why Spring was willing to go with Bert to Bolivia. She knew why Autumn had waited eight years to have Nathan.

Her mind at ease, Summer leaned back and slept until she felt a hand on her shoulder. She looked up into David's concerned face.

"Why, David," she said, "how did you know?"

"Edna telephoned me as soon as you went looking for Timmy. I started home then, and she told me she would stay in her office if I wanted to contact her again. I stopped for gas a few hours ago, and learned you'd brought Timmy to the hospital." He knelt beside her. "How is he?"

"His arm is broken, but the doctor thinks that's all. If he's okay, they'll send him home this morning."

"You look like you've had a hard night."

She looked down at her muddy, wrinkled garments, and told David all that happened.

"I couldn't have done better," he said. "I'll take the boys and Anita to The Crossroads, and then come right back to you." He brushed back her hair and massaged the tight muscles in her neck and shoulders. "I'll take my share of the load now."

Summer stayed home with Timmy for several days, but when the pain was gone, he went back to kindergarten, and she went to work. The mission board required a lot of reports at the end of the school term, and she needed to get started on them.

Her first day back, Summer looked up when a knock sounded at the office door. A postman entered carrying a large box.

"I've got a parcel here for the family of Bert and Spring Brown in care of The Crossroads. They live here?"

Summer swallowed, finding it difficult to answer. "No. They're deceased. I'm Spring Brown's sister."

"That's family as far as I'm concerned," the postman said. He set the parcel beside Summer's desk and pulled a few papers off the top of the box. Pushing the papers toward Summer, he said, "Sign here, ma'am."

She glanced at the name of the sender—a garage in Scranton, Pennsylvania! Summer automatically signed her name. The man thanked her and exited. She sat stunned until she heard the postman's van driving away.

"David! Come here," she yelled in a loud, raspy voice. He rushed into the room.

"What is it?"

She pointed to the box. His face turned white when he read the address label.

"What could be in it?" Summer whispered, bewildered.

"It has to be something that belonged to Bert and Spring. During all our sorrow over their deaths and our move to The Crossroads, I didn't even think that Bert and Spring would have had luggage in their car when they had the accident. There's no other explanation for this box. If I had thought about it, I probably would have figured everything was destroyed. It was a terrible wreck."

"I can't bear to open it."

"It won't be easy, but we have to see what's in it."

He pulled a small penknife from his pocket.

"Just a minute, David. Let me think." Summer lifted a hand to her pulsating throat. "Timmy and Nicole seem to have accepted their parents' deaths, but once in a while I hear something that sounds as if they might still expect them to come home. Should the children be with us when we open the box? It will be painful for them, but it might be what's needed for them to face reality."

David nodded his head. "You're right. When should we do it?"

"As soon as possible. I can't stand procrastination."

David smiled. "I like to put off unpleasant things, but I am curious. We'll do it tonight."

David carried the box to the cabin and put it in the closet. After Nicole and Timmy performed their assigned chores to remove the dishes from the table, stacking them in the sink, and taking the garbage to the outside can, they settled in front of the television as usual.

Summer ran water into the sink and soaked the dishes in warm suds. David picked up a dishcloth, leaned against the cabinet, and dried the dishes. Summer was hardly aware of what her hands were doing. Memories of Spring and the days of their childhood in Ohio were both painful and cleansing. Somehow she knew this box was the last tangible tie she'd have of her sister.

When David put the last plate and glass in the cabinet, with a glance at the children, he said, "I guess we can't wait any longer."

"That program will be over in ten minutes."

David sat beside Timmy and Nicole on the sofa. When the program had almost ended, he went to the closet and removed the box.

"Whatcha got, Uncle David?" Timmy called as David sat on the fireplace ledge and placed the box in front of him.

"We'll find out in a little bit."

When the cartoon ended, Timmy ran to David. "Is it a present?"

"I don't know. We'll have to open the box to find out."

Timmy and Nicole crowded close to David and he put his arm around them. With an apologetic glance at Summer, he said quietly, "Maybe you'd better open it."

Bringing a sharp knife from a kitchen cabinet, Summer's hands halted momentarily over the box, fearful of what trouble the next few minutes might bring.

While she hesitated, David explained, "This box

came today from a garage in Pennsylvania, and it's addressed to the family of Bert and Spring Brown."

Nicole clapped her hands. "That's us. See, I've been telling you, Timmy, that Mommy and Daddy are still alive. They've sent us a package."

The courage that Summer had been building up since the box arrived disappeared completely. Tears glistened in David's eyes and he shook his head. He was beyond speech, so it was up to her.

"This box was sent from the garage that towed in your parents' car after the automobile accident." Hope slowly faded from Nicole's face as Summer continued, "We think it may be the luggage they had with them, but we waited until the four of us were together to find out."

Summer cut the tape on the box and lifted the lid. An envelope lay on top of the contents. She opened it and read aloud.

"'The contents of this box were found in the wrecked automobile registered to Bert Brown. The suitcases were destroyed, but we picked up some items that were salvageable. Pardon our delay in sending these possessions. We had laid them aside expecting someone to call for them and, today, one of our staff members discovered the box.'"

Summer lifted the items one by one—a briefcase, a purse, a few books and a Bible. Before she reached the bottom of the box, both children were bawling and tears dripped from David's eyes. Summer was almost at the breaking point, but someone had to stay calm, so she rallied all the Weaver stamina she possessed.

When she lifted out the Bible, Nicole sobbed, "That's Daddy's Bible. He wouldn't go anyplace without it, so he didn't go to Bolivia. He's not coming back. They *are* dead."

When she laid Bert's Bible on an end table, two envelopes fell out of it. One of the envelopes had her name and complete New York mailing address on it, and the other was addressed to David in Atlanta. Both envelopes were stamped. She stuck them in the pocket of her slacks.

Timmy groveled on the floor, kicking his feet and crying, "I want my daddy and mommy." Nicole wrapped her arms around the Bible. David reached for his handkerchief and blew his nose.

"Daddy's coming home. He is coming home, Uncle David! I know he is," Timmy said.

David sat on the floor and tried to draw the struggling child into his arms, but Timmy kept shoving him away.

"No, Timmy, your daddy has gone to Heaven. He won't come back to The Crossroads."

"Don't he love us anymore?"

David threw a helpless look toward Summer, saying, "He'll always love you. For some reason, Jesus was ready for Bert and Spring to come to live with Him. I don't know why, but that's where they are now."

"Where is Heaven? If they won't come back to us, we'll go where they are," Nicole said.

"Someday you'll go to see your parents," David insisted, "but it may not be for a long time. Until then, you just have to go on living the way your parents would want you to live."

"We're orphans," Nicole moaned. "Just like some of the kids at school. We don't have any parents."

"You do have parents," Summer said firmly. "David and I are your parents now. You're luckier than lots of kids, who only have one set of parents.''

David threw her an approving smile.

It took more than two hours to console the children and get them settled into bed. Summer had never been so exhausted in her life. When they returned to the kitchen area, David got a can of soda from the refrigerator. He poured the contents over two glasses of ice, handed one to Summer, and dropped wearily on the couch.

''I've been through a lot of bad experiences in my life, but nothing like this,'' David said.

''And we aren't finished yet,'' Summer said as she took the two envelopes from her pocket. She handed David the envelope addressed to him. ''There were two letters in that box—one for each of us.''

They opened them at the same time. The messages were identical, dated a few days before Spring and Bert had died.

Dear Summer and David,

For the past few weeks we've felt compelled to make our wills. We don't have much in the way of material possessions, unless we consider that Spring might someday inherit one third of the Weaver estate. Our most prized possessions are our children. We've been trying for days to decide who to ask to assume responsibility for them if we should die before the children are grown. We realize we're asking a great deal of you, but after praying for several days about it, God has repeatedly brought your names to mind. Will you be willing for us to appoint you as co-guardians of Timmy and Nicole? And will you move to The Crossroads and bring the children up in our home there? This would involve a big sacrifice, but both of us believe that you're the ones to care for our children and the work we've started in North Carolina. We're very concerned about your lack of spiritual commitment, and living at The Crossroads might bring about a change in your lives. Please let us know if you'll accept this responsibility. If you won't, we will understand and make other arrangements. This isn't a decision for you to take lightly. We'll be praying for God's will to be done. We love you.

Bert and Spring

Summer twisted the letter in her hand. David cleared his throat. "I feel better to know they'd intended to give us a choice in the matter," he said.

"I wonder if I'd have agreed to their requests if I'd gotten this letter before they died. I don't think I would have."

"I feel sure I'd have said no. Fate intervened before I could give my answer."

"Do you think *fate* is the right word?" Summer asked, a smile trembling on her lips.

"No, of course not. Although I still don't understand why God didn't choose to save Bert and Spring in that accident, I believe it's His will for us to be at The Crossroads."

"I believe that, too, but I'm not sure whether He wants us here for a year or a lifetime," Summer answered quietly.

"But wherever we are, I'm convinced that God wants us to be together. I've been trying to get this out for weeks, and I'm not going to delay any longer.

I love you, Summer. Do you care enough for me to become my wife?''

"I've been fighting this decision, but the other night in the hospital, I knew that I want to spend the rest of my life with you wherever God wants us to live. There have been times when I've thought I couldn't love anybody, but I love Timmy and Nicole, and I love you, too, but in a much different way.''

"I should hope so,'' he said playfully. All his concerns that Summer could ever love him were gone. He stood and pulled her upward into his arms. There was a stirring intimacy to his kiss now that he had suppressed before. His lips lingered and Summer savored every moment of his caress. Her eyes glowed with enjoyment when she lifted her head and her lips nibbled the curve of his handsome profile.

"I've been so troubled the past few months over the promise I made Spring, that I thought I'd never make another one. But there's one more promise I want to make as soon as possible.''

Mimicking the deep tones of a minister, Summer said, '''Will you take this man to be your wedded husband, to live together in the holy estate of matrimony? Will you love him, comfort him, honor and keep him, in sickness and in health, and forsaking all others keep yourself unto him only as long as you both shall live?'''

David's smile was as intimate as a kiss when he prompted, "The woman shall answer...''

With her lips hovering near his, Summer promised, "I will.''

Epilogue

For the third time, the gazebo at the Weaver farmstead was decorated for a wedding. From the window of her room on the second floor, Summer, dressed in a white silk gown, watched her father approach the house driving a black barouche pulled by two Belgian horses. She and David had arrived at the farm a week ago with Timmy and Nicole.

A year had passed since they'd moved to North Carolina, bringing significant changes in their lives. She and David had been appointed legal guardians for Timmy and Nicole, and a few weeks ago, they'd also accepted permanent appointments at The Crossroads.

Their dreams to place The Crossroads on a self-supporting basis hadn't yet materialized although the newsletter had prompted a few people to make sizeable contributions to the school. They'd accepted the appointments on faith just as Edna and their siblings had done. Once she and David had made the decision to marry and to stay at The Crossroads, Summer had never looked back.

In the distance, Summer could see the cemetery where Bert and Spring were buried. Did they know that today she and David were getting married and that they'd agreed to carry on the work at The Crossroads? She believed they did.

The day before, she and David had walked with Timmy and Nicole to the cemetery, and they'd all knelt beside the graves of Bert and Spring to make their final goodbyes. It had been a tearful time for the four of them but, after a good cry, even the children seemed ready to cut their ties with the past.

A knock sounded at the door and Summer forgot the past to rejoice in the present. The time for reminiscing was over. Her sister, Autumn, entered with Timmy and Nicole in tow.

"Oh," Nicole breathed. "You're so pretty, Auntie. No wonder Uncle David loves you so much."

Summer and Autumn exchanged amused glances, but Summer's eyes brightened with tenderness and love, when Nicole said, "We'll always remember Mommy and Daddy, but Timmy and me...well, now that you and Uncle David are getting married, would it be all right if we call you Mom and Dad?"

"We want to be your kids," Timmy added.

Summer's voluminous skirt swirled around her when she knelt and gathered the two children into her arms. "There's nothing we'd like better. We already think of you as our children, but we'll make it legal so you'll have the right to call us Mom and Dad."

She and David had talked about adopting the children, but they hadn't wanted to supplant Spring and Bert in the children's memories. But since Nicole and

Timmy had taken the initiative, they'd go ahead immediately with adoption procedures.

"Time to go," Landon Weaver called through the open window.

Autumn helped Summer to stand and arranged the long skirt behind her sister. Summer took the hands of Nicole and Timmy and started down the broad stairway.

They joined Landon in the barouche, and in a short time reached the flower-decorated gazebo. Summer took Landon's arm, and her attention focused on David standing a few feet away, his brown eyes alight with pleasure and tenderness. They exchanged secret smiles, and eagerness marked Summer's steps as she moved to his side. She had another promise to make and to keep.

* * * * *

Dear Reader,

It may be difficult for you to believe that the heroine of this book could have spent over thirty years of her life without having any knowledge of the Christian faith. But after I'd created Summer Weaver as a character, a young woman of thirty-four came to our church and immediately accepted Christ as her Savior. Although she'd lived in a section of our state that has many churches, the only Christian services she'd attended were a few funerals. Without any knowledge of the Bible, she was drawn to the faith through the working of the Holy Spirit.

Over the past few years, as I've worked with youth in our local church, I'm frequently pleased at how rapidly individuals can mature in their spiritual walk with God when they have the desire to do so. Miracles take place when God works through a committed person, as exemplified by the spiritual growth of David Brown and Summer Weaver in *Summer's Promise*. I pray that this book will influence each reader to examine his/her relationship to Christ and submit to His Lordship.

Mail from readers is always encouraging when I realize that through my writing, individuals are quickened to a closer walk with God. To quote from a recent letter: "God can use any venue to bring about understanding of the Scriptures. I personally thank Him that He offers those of us who love romances an alternative. May God keep using you as a voice crying out in the literary wilderness."

I send out a semiannual newsletter, and if you'd like to receive copies, please let me know at P.O. Box 2770, Southside, West Virginia, 25187.

Irene B. Brand

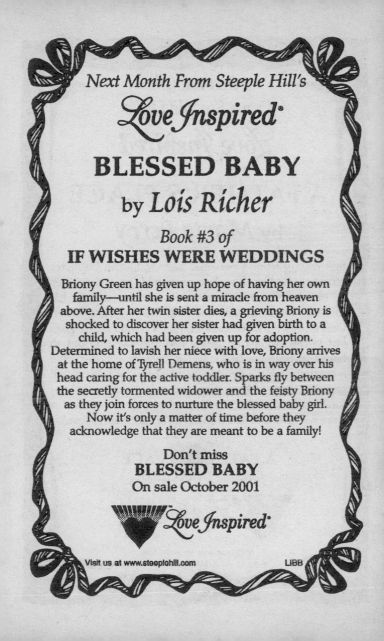

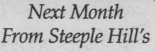

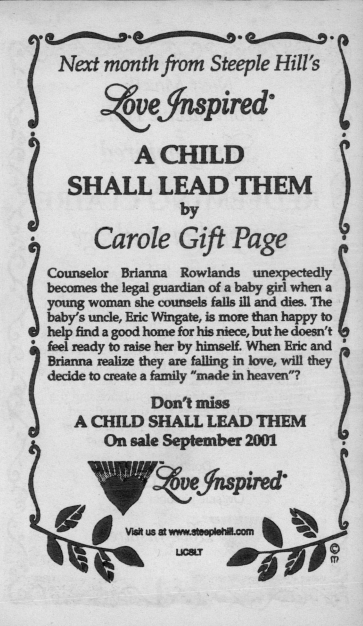

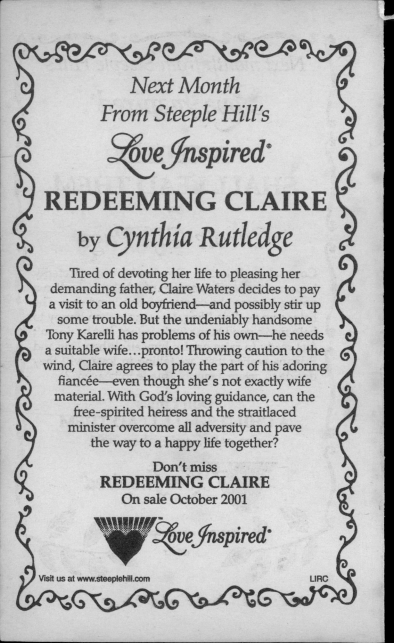